The Reunion

Look for other **ANIMORPHS**®
titles by K.A. Applegate:

the andalite chronicles

The Hork-Bajir Chronicles

ALTERNAMORPHS
The First Journey

ANIMORPHS ®

The Reunion

K.A. Applegate

AN
APPLE
PAPERBACK

SCHOLASTIC INC.
New York Toronto London Auckland Sydney
Mexico City New Delhi Hong Kong

Cover illustration by David B. Mattingly

No part of this publication may be reproduced in whole or in part, or stored in a retrieval system, or transmitted in any form or by any means, electronic, mechanical, photocopying, recording, or otherwise, without written permission of the publisher. For information regarding permission, write to Scholastic Inc., Attention: Permissions Department, 555 Broadway, New York, NY 10012.

ISBN 0-590-76263-X

12 11 10 9 8 7 6 5 4 3 2 1   9/9 0 1 2 3 4/0

Printed in the U.S.A.   40

First Scholastic printing, June 1999

The author wishes to thank Elise Donner
for her help in preparing this manuscript.

For Michael and Jake

The Reunion

CHAPTER 1

It was happening again. Unbelievably, it was happening again.

A woman was drowning. Not the dreaded leader of an alien force. Just a woman. Alone in a roiling sea. Defenseless. Vulnerable.

My mother.

There was no way I could let it happen again.

I powered toward her. My arms strained with each stroke. My legs kicked wildly.

Hold on. Hold on!

So close. Close enough to see her straining to keep her head above the cold black water.

Then I was on her, one arm around her shoulders, the other paddling madly to keep us afloat.

"Hold on!" I cried. "I've got you!"

1

She looked up at me, wet hair plastering her face. Then she spoke. "Thank you, Marco."

"Mom . . ."

"I'm free, Marco. I'm free!"

And then a powerful current swept her out of my grasp and sucked her under the glittering surface of the midnight ocean.

"No! No, no, no!"

I dove. The salt stung my eyes. I pushed deeper and deeper into the darkness. My lungs ached but I would not allow it to happen again. I would not let her go! Not when she was free. Not . . .

"NO!"

"Marco? Are you okay?"

I shot up straight as a board. Where . . . ? My bed, my room. My father.

I put my hands to my head and looked at the picture of my mother that sat on my nightstand.

"You okay?" he repeated.

No. I wasn't. "Yeah. Yeah. Bad dream, I guess."

"About her?"

I swallowed hard. "Yeah."

Dad sat on the edge of my bed and hugged me.

I returned the hug weakly. Patted him on the back.

"I'm okay, big guy," I said. "What time is it?"

2

"About time to get up and get going," he said. "I get the shower first. I have to be in early today."

I watched my father leave the room. But instead of getting out of bed and heading downstairs for a bowl of Honeycomb, I sat amidst the tangled, slightly damp bedcovers, too exhausted to move.

My name, as you probably know by now, is Marco. And that was how my Friday started. Not the greatest way to greet the last day of a long week. But not exactly uncommon. Dreams of fear and loss and despair.

Before I lost my mother to the enemy, before I learned of the Yeerk invasion of Earth, my life was pretty tame. Mostly I worried about things like whether I'd dropped enough hints at dinner about which Sega disk I wanted for my birthday.

Not about things like the enslavement of the human race.

Those were the days. Or, as Dad says, "The salad days."

I'm not sure what that means exactly — "salad days" — but he says it a lot. I'm not a big fan of salad myself, unless it's heavily croutoned.

Anyway, here's the rough sequence of events. I'll keep it brief.

My mother — my beautiful, pretty-smelling, intelligent mother — took our boat out late one night and never came back. They found the boat. They didn't find her.

She was presumed drowned. With no explanation of why she had done such a strange thing like take the boat out alone. At night. I mean, my mother was not exactly the suicidal type.

Next. My friends — Jake, Rachel, Cassie, and Tobias — and I had the distinct misfortune to stumble upon a dying Andalite warrior prince who told us about the Yeerks and their invasion of our planet. He gave us the gift and curse of morphing, an Andalite technology that allows us to acquire the DNA of any animal and become — morph — that animal.

This is our most spectacular weapon. The others are cunning, courage, and secrecy. (And in my case irresistible cuteness.)

Then, we were joined by Aximili-Esgarrouth-Isthill, younger brother of Prince Elfangor.

Another highlight. This happened long after I'd learned my mother had not fallen overboard and drowned but had been infested by the Yeerk known as Visser One, originator of the Earth invasion. I'm talking about the time I'd seen her frail, Yeerk-infested body floating facedown as the Yeerks' underwater headquarters destructed.

Since that moment I've spent at least, oh, a

bazillion hours wondering if my mother could have survived. Rachel heard a submarine speeding away from the chaotic scene. And I'd seen a Leeran-Controller swimming toward my mother's floating body. So there was a chance she'd lived, a chance the Leeran had dragged her unconscious body to the sub and powered away.

At least, that's what I chose to believe. But alongside that belief was the realization that the chances she'd made it to the sub were slim.

You can understand how sometimes my particular daily grind gets to be a pain in the . . .

I mean, five more or less normal kids, one of whom is now more bird than boy, plus an Andalite cadet are supposed to save the Earth from an army of evil sluglike parasites?

What are the odds that's going to happen?

The Yeerks are parasitic. They squirm their way into your ear canal and from there seep into every nook and cranny of your brain. They assume total control over your thoughts and your actions. They leave you alert and alive — but absolutely powerless to act or speak on your own behalf. You are locked in a kind of brain cage while the Yeerk takes over every single aspect of your life. The Yeerk is in total control.

Total control.

The Yeerk moves your eyes and hands and

5

feet. The Yeerk speaks with your voice. The Yeerk opens your memories and reads them like a book. Every memory. Every secret.

The Yeerk in my mother's head can look through her memories and see what she saw as she comforted me in my crib long, long ago. The Yeerk can see memories of me crying from a skinned knee. Memories of grouchy breakfasts with my dad and me. Memories of the hideously embarrassing "birds and bees" conversation.

The Yeerk saw all of that. The Yeerk who held the rank of Visser One. The original overlord of the invasion of Earth. The Yeerk who made a slave of my mother.

Because of this invasion our lives have become a series of fierce battles and narrow escapes. Of soul-crushing experiences and bone-shattering fights. You can see why my mornings have taken a dramatic turn for the worse.

Just the same, when Dad left for work, I took a shower and got ready with every intention of going to school.

Really, I did.

CHAPTER 2

With a clean face and conditioned hair I headed toward the school bus stop.

And walked past it.

Instead, I hopped on a city bus headed downtown.

The warren of streets that is the financial and business center of our town seemed as good a place as any to kill time. To get lost without running the risk of running into anyone who knew me.

There were movie theaters downtown. I figured I'd look around till I could catch a matinee of something loud and fun.

Twenty minutes later the bus dropped me and

thirty office-bound men and women in the heart of blue-suit central.

It was still way early but already the sun was heating up the sidewalks, and the exhaust from the cars, trucks, and buses was spread like a grubby, smelly blanket over the concrete and steel jungle.

Nice choice, Marco. I should have gone to the beach. I stood on the sidewalk and stared.

Seething mass of humanity. I'd heard that phrase once and now I knew what it meant. It meant "office workers at rush hour."

What was the big hurry? Did adults really like going to work? Or was Friday free donut day at the office?

THWACK!

I was down! My knees hit the pavement and my face landed in a planter full of cigarette butts and abandoned coffee cups.

The enemy! I prepared myself for the next blow.

Nothing. I looked up.

No one had noticed I'd been knocked over.

I got to my feet, dazed. I rubbed the ash, dirt, and stale coffee off my face with the bottom of my shirt.

I was disgusted. And I was mad.

A woman had run me over with her tank of a briefcase. Then she'd continued on down the street like nothing had happened. And no one had stopped to help me.

"And they say *my* generation has no manners," I muttered.

I gave myself a quick once-over — nothing seriously damaged but my dignity — and set out after the woman who'd so callously whacked me. This woman had an appointment with the dirty pavement, courtesy of a well-placed Saucony Cross Trainer.

I caught up to her about halfway down the block and followed a few feet behind. Waiting for my chance. Her briefcase was big enough to hold a Doberman and built to maim, with steel corners and a big combination lock on the side.

And what was up with that hair? The woman wore a stiff, curly blonde wig. Think steel-wool pad. Used. Slightly shredded. And yellow.

I saw the perfect spot to exact my revenge.

I skirted the crowd and hid behind a big, concrete column about a yard ahead, just at the corner of the courthouse. When Wig Lady passed — bingo, bango! BAM!

She was going down.

I peeked from around the pillar to see how close she was to meeting my foot. And then I bit my cheek to stop from screaming.

The woman with the awful blonde hair and the briefcase . . .

9

Was my mother!

Visser One!

I ducked back behind the column and pulled my South Park cap down over my eyes. She passed by. She hadn't seen me.

My mother was alive!

I took a deep breath and tried to comprehend this fact. She'd escaped the destruction of the Yeerk underwater complex. Relief and happiness and fear all at once. She was alive! But she was so dangerous. So terribly dangerous.

Think, Marco. She's alive, but . . . the disguise. A blue power suit. A curly blonde wig. What had looked like blue contact lenses behind big, black-rimmed glasses. The massive brief-case.

Why a disguise? To hide. From whom?

Should I follow her? Find the others? I could still make it to school before the late bell. Maybe.

But then I'd lose my mother for sure. And Visser One.

I watched my mother's body walk down the street. When she reached the next corner, I followed.

On the next block I saw her climb the steps to the front doors of the Sutherland Tower, the downtown area's tallest building. She squeezed herself and her briefcase into a compartment of the revolving door. I bolted up the steps, waited one extra revolution of the brass-plated door, then followed her in.

The lobby was about three stories tall. Behind a row of security guards, water flowed down one pink marble wall into a lit pool. Visser One flashed some kind of pass and continued by the guard's station.

I had no pass. Plus I was a kid. The guards had already seen me come in, and now they were looking at me like I was one hundred percent no-good. If I made the wrong move they were sure to hassle me. Then the Visser would look over her shoulder to see what the commotion was about and I'd be in big, big trouble.

Visser One would recognize me as her host body's son.

So I stood. Just stopped right there by the revolving door and waited for the next person to come through.

Whoever it was, their DNA was mine.

CHAPTER 3

The revolving door whooshed. Footsteps behind me. I turned around.

"Hi, Dad!" I said. "What took you so long?"

The man was stocky, well-dressed, and surprised. But he had his ID in one hand and I had his other hand and before he knew it, the mild acquisition trance was in place.

"Hello, Mr. Grant," said a slick-haired security guard.

"It's 'Fathers Take Their Sons to Work Day!'" I said brightly as I led the zoned-out Mr. Grant past security.

"Well, then, son, you pay attention! That's one important daddy you got!"

"Yessir!" I replied.

12

The boyish enthusiasm worked like a charm. I've found that if you act like a moron, adults tend to leave you alone. It's when they think you might be as smart as they are that they give you a hard time.

I led Mr. Grant to the elevator. Let me make it clear that I had no intention of morphing this man. I just needed him to get me past security and to the elevators.

Where Visser One was standing with her enormous metal case.

Mr. Grant was waking up. I let go of his hand.

"My," he muttered, putting his hand on his stomach. "That jelly donut is not sitting well."

I looked up at Mr. Grant with an Adam Sandler idiot grin.

Worked like a charm. Mr. Grant looked away and waited impatiently for the elevator with the rest of the men and woman in suits.

I pulled my hat lower over my face.

DING! The elevator door opened. An old guy with a rolling cart full of interoffice envelopes and UPS packages made an attempt to get out of the car.

"Let 'em off, people!" he muttered as the crowd surged around him and into the elevator.

Visser One passed on the mail guy's right. I went to his left. The mob prevented her from getting a glimpse of me.

The doors closed. We were packed in the elevator like crayons in a crayon box. The important thing was Visser One was the crayon close to the button panel, and I was the crayon in the opposite back corner.

But that's not good, I thought suddenly. I have to get out when my mom . . . the Visser gets out! If I miss the floor, I lose the Visser. And my mother. Again.

At the same time, I couldn't allow Visser One to see me. There was only one thing I could do. A morph. In the slow-moving elevator. Surrounded by fifteen people and evil incarnate.

A woman whose back was about three inches from the bill of my baseball cap dropped a section of her *Wall Street Journal* and I pretended not to notice. I slid down against the elevator wall, back straight, and with my fingertips, picked it up off the grubby red carpet. Behind the suited backs of fifteen adults, I opened the paper as wide as I could and held it in front of my face and over my head, like a tent. And then I began one of my least favorite morphs — the common housefly.

Insane! It was insane. But what was my other choice? Lose Visser One? No. Not happening.

I started shrinking almost immediately. In a moment, the newspaper blanketed me. My vision went dark and then flashed on again, pixilated.

Two fly legs spurted from my chest. My hands shriveled into pincers. My skin hardened.

And nobody noticed. It was bizarre! No one looked at me. Everyone continued to stare blankly ahead at the door or up at the ventilation grates on the roof of the elevator car.

I was in an elevator full of people, turning into a fly, and no one so much as glanced back at me. I fought down the lunatic urge to say, "Hey, I'm turning into a fly, here. Hello? Are you people or statues?"

The elevator slowed and stopped at a floor. The woman who had dropped the paper earlier bent to pick it up.

Problem. I wasn't done morphing!

I was about the size of a rat, with pink skin and a human nose. The other nine-tenths of me was housefly. Wings, six hairy legs, compound eyes, a big sticky tongue where my mouth had been. And I was sitting in the middle of a mound of clothes.

A more disgusting sight I cannot imagine.

The woman picked up the paper, stared back at a piece of nothing two feet above the head of the person in front of her, then froze.

"Argh!" she said.

Through my 360-degree multifaceted fly vision I watched her look slowly back down to the dirty red carpet. But it was too late.

Totally fly now, I kicked on my wings, zoomed crazily into the air, sped over the woman's head and landed on a corner of the Visser's briefcase. The elevator door opened. The woman who was positive she had just seen a rat-sized fly-boy on the elevator floor rushed out with her hand to her mouth.

A few other business people filed out after her and the Visser pressed the CLOSE button.

The twenty-first floor. Mr. Grant got off.

The Visser pushed CLOSE once more.

And I was alone in the elevator with my mother.

Twenty-second floor. The elevator slid to a stop. The doors opened and Visser One stepped out into the hallway. I rode on her briefcase to where she stopped just outside the third door on the right.

It was all I needed to know. Time to get out of there and tell the others.

CHAPTER 4

I let go with my sticky, pincher fly feet. I buzzed my gossamer wings and lifted up off the Visser's metal case.

Up, circle back and away toward . . .

SCHLOOOOP!

Wind! A tornado of wind!

My wings beat with a speed only an insect could achieve. But I was too close! A vent, ribbed steel, as high as a ten-story building to me, and twice as wide.

Air cleaner! Industrial-strength. Suction. Suction like a vacuum cleaner!

WHAM!

I hit a metal crossbar.

Then I was through. Hurtling down an aluminum shaft. And now, concentrated in the enclosed space, the air current was unbelievable.

<Aaaagh!>

I was spinning, out of control, wings almost useless. And I wasn't alone. Pieces of lint and human hair. Dust and the circles of paper a three-hole puncher leaves behind. An assortment of dazed mosquitoes, gnats, and other flies, all zooming around me like the tornado scene from *The Wizard of Oz.* All of it shattered into the thousand tiny TV sets of my fly eyes. All of it in weird, distorted colors.

I tumbled faster and faster toward a giant filter. Bundles of flying-bug parts and lint were scattered at its base. There was only one thing to do.

Demorph!

I started growing almost immediately and almost immediately I stopped tumbling. Anything over the weight of a flicked booger pretty much canceled out the power of the industrial-strength air cleaner.

My wings shriveled and sucked into the now-supple skin under my shoulder blades. My eyes rotated from the sides of my head back to the front of my face. Two fly legs shot back into my chest.

FLOOP! FLOOP!

My other fly legs rotated to where my human

legs and arms should be and everything started to grow. Suddenly, I realized that the aluminum shaft that had seemed as big as the school gym when I was a fly just might not be big enough for my human self.

Getting trapped like a big chunk of Snicker's Blizzard in a straw was something I was not prepared for.

I pushed my now-human arms in front of me and thrust my legs behind me. I lay fully extended on my stomach in the air shaft.

And then I stopped demorphing. I was me. For once, I was grateful to be a little on the short side.

Still, I was trapped inside a very dusty air vent.

I slithered down the square metal tube, away from the filter, toward a light beaming across the shaft. I pushed myself forward with my toes and pulled myself along with my fingers, trying hard not to panic.

The light was coming from a vent high on the wall of an office. I gave the grate a whack and it opened downward like a miniature door. I was a good eight or nine feet in the air. I lowered myself headfirst, slowly, slowly . . .

Keys jingled outside the door.

I dropped fast, forcing myself into a head-over-heels tumble as I fell.

BAM!

Right into a wastebasket.

"Three points," I whispered to myself.

The door to the office opened just as I scurried into the second room, a big, windowless space full of gray cubicles.

"Hello?" Lights popped on. "Mr. Grant?"

Footsteps. Slow, but coming my way.

I had no choice! I had to morph Mr. Grant.

I dashed into an empty cubicle at the back of the room and felt the changes begin.

Morphing a fly may be gross, but morphing a human being is far more frightening. Not to mention morally suspect. In this case, morphing an adult male was like getting an unwanted glimpse into my own future and realizing that my future was not pretty.

The first thing to change was my stomach. It grew out and around until the seams of my morphing suit began to tear.

My thick, gorgeous hair was sucked into my broadening skull. I slapped a hand to my head. A receding hairline! A balding spot right on top!

I watched as the skin on my hands wrinkled slightly. Pale blotches sprinkled themselves across the knuckles. I touched my face with the ugly fingers. Wow! Rough . . . At this rate I'd have a five o'clock shadow by noon!

Riiiiip!

My butt! I turned my double-chinned neck as far as it would turn and saw over my thick shoulder a wide protuberance — and my bike shorts in shreds.

Panic set in. I was pretty sure I hadn't grown taller but man, had I gotten wider!

"Mr. Grant?"

"Yes?" I yelped, sticking my balding, slightly grizzled head over the cubicle partition.

The woman stood in the doorway of the second room.

"Uh, are you okay, Mr. Grant?" She took another step inside.

"No!" I shouted. "I mean, don't come in. I'm very busy. I'm just fine."

"You were working in the dark Mr. Grant. Are you sure . . ."

"Yes, I'm just fine, thanks. I'll be done here in a few minutes," I babbled.

Another step closer. "Why are you at Carlos's desk?"

Good one. I thought fast. "Uh, well, there's something wrong with my computer, so, uh, I thought I'd borrow this one. Uh, could you get me a cup of coffee from the Starbucks on the corner? Please?"

The woman's eyebrows quirked but she turned and headed for the door. "Sure, Mr. Grant. I'll be right back."

"Thanks, thanks a lot!" I said, ducking back behind the cubicle partition.

Yow! Too close. I waited until I hoped the woman had gotten on the elevator and sprinted from the cubicle. Time to find a place safe to demorph and get the heck out of this building.

The men's room. I flung open the door to the hallway. And ran smack into . . .

"Aaahh!" I yelled. "Mr. Grant!"

"What the . . ." was all he got out before he slumped to the floor.

I shot a glance up and down the hallway. No one.

"Oh man, oh man, Jake is gonna kill me, and if *he* doesn't, Cassie will." I hefted Mr. Grant to a half-sitting position and dragged him across the hall and into a broom closet. It was like moving one of those stones they used to build the pyramids. The man liked his pastry.

I shut the door behind us and tried to catch my breath. Hard to do when you're panicking on several fronts simultaneously.

I propped him up against a mop bucket on wheels and started to undress him.

Quickly, I changed into Mr. Grant's blue suit. Well, all except the tie. I have no idea how to tie one.

When I was dressed I opened the broom closet

door, looked both ways, then scooted as fast as Mr. Grant could to the elevator.

A moment later the elevator doors slid open and I burst inside.

I was outta there.

CHAPTER 5

It was almost lunch period by the time I'd gone home, changed, and got back to school.

Now, getting into school late is not the easiest thing in the world to do, but it can be done. Luckily, our school has no guards or metal detectors like they have in the high schools. All I had to worry about was the stray teacher or kiss-up hall monitor.

I leaned around the front door. Nobody. Just the janitor, but his back was to me and he was wearing headphones. And doing this weird kind of shuffling dance as he pushed a mop across the vomit-green linoleum tile that is our school's main hallway.

I slid around the doorjamb and booked the

other way down the main hall. I could see the tops of teachers' heads through the windows in the classroom doors, but knew they couldn't see me. Another benefit of being vertically challenged.

I made it to my locker undetected. A second later, the bell for lunch period rang and the halls were mobbed by kids charging out of class. One of them was Jake. I dropped my math book. He picked it up.

"Jake, you really do care."

"Where have you been?" he demanded.

"Guess who I saw?" I whispered, pulling a notebook at random from my locker.

Jake sighed. "Marco, just tell me . . ."

"Marco!"

A hand clapped onto my shoulder.

"So nice of you to join us today."

"My pleasure, Mr. Chapman," I said. "I would never want to miss a day of learning."

Jake gave me a "This-is-*your*-problem" look and sauntered away.

"Ah, amusing as always, Marco. And where might you have been? I called your home. No answer. No answer at all."

"I was . . . with my father."

"Oh, really?"

"Yes, Mr. Chapman. It was 'Take Your Son to Work Day' at his office."

"Then I suppose you won't mind me calling him at work?"

"Not at all," I bluffed. "Would you like the number?"

Chapman looked me up and down. If he called my dad, I was busted, big time.

"He'll be in meetings all afternoon, that's why I came back to school," I added. "But you could leave a message on his voice mail."

"Just get where you're supposed to be, Marco."

"Yes, sir."

I should have said "Yes, you Yeerk-carrying freak." But that would have been fatal. To me.

Telling Jake about Visser One would have to wait. In the cafeteria I passed a note to Rachel.

Barn. After school. Good news and bad.

I sat at the end of a lunch table and ate my pizza alone.

Ignored the minor food fight going on at the table to my right. Vaguely noticed the pimply kid slurping some gross yellow soup from a plaid thermos at the other end of my table. Thought for two seconds about the history test I was going to fail that afternoon. Wondered if Chapman was going to bring up my cutting school and failing my history test at the next parent-teacher conference. Considered whether I'd rather spend my life working at McDonald's or Burger King after I got expelled.

But my mind wouldn't stay on any one topic. Nothing really mattered, did it? Nothing except one extraordinarily complicated, amazingly wonderful fact.

My mother was alive.

Alive.

I saw Rachel giving me the fish eye from across the room. I mouthed that one word: *alive.*

Evidently Rachel doesn't read lips. She misunderstood what I'd said and responded by mouthing two words I won't repeat.

But I didn't care. No one could blow this one moment of relief for me.

She was alive. And someday, somehow, by some miracle I could only fantasize about, she'd be my mom again.

CHAPTER 6

"Marco," Cassie said, "tell us why we're here."

"We" being four kids, a bird, and a furry blue alien. Freaks is our name, saving the world is our game.

"This morning I skipped school and took the bus downtown." I shot a look at Jake. "And before anyone jumps down my throat, I know it's dumb to call attention to myself, so sue me. Anyway, I was trying to avoid being trampled by the wing tips when I saw my . . . Visser One. She was in disguise. A terrible wig, blue contacts, and big square glasses. But it was her."

"Oh, man," Jake said. "Are you sure it was your mother?"

28

"Oh, yeah. I got a great look at her right before I was going to trip her."

"You were going to trip your mother?" said Cassie.

"Yes, because she'd knocked me down with this big metal briefcase. It doesn't matter. What matters is that it was Visser One. My mother. In disguise."

"You're sure she didn't recognize you and knock you down on purpose?" Rachel demanded.

"Yeah," I said. "Anyway, she thinks I'm a Controller. Remember when we went after the Yeerks' underwater complex? Don't forget: We spoke. She thinks I'm one of them. So why would she smack me, unprovoked? And if she knew the truth about me, she'd have done more than just knock me down."

"And what *was* the brilliant motive behind skipping school?"

"I'm an adventurer, Rachel," I said. "Much like Daniel Boone. Magellan. Marco Polo. I will not rest until I have explored every alley, every nook, every cranny of this big, crazy world of ours."

"Not funny, Mr. Polo," she snapped. "You could have gotten us in big trouble. . . ."

<What is a cranny, exactly?> Tobias wondered from his perch above us.

<So. Visser One is alive,> Ax said coldly. <This is not good news.>

29

"The corollary, Ax. My mother's alive, too," I pointed out. "I followed her into the Sutherland Tower. She's got an office on the twenty-second floor."

"What do you think she's doing in there?" Cassie said.

I shook my head. "I didn't stick around to find out."

"The last time we saw Visser One," Jake mused, "Visser Three saw us — the enemy — spare her life."

<If Visser Three understood that we spared Visser One, he would conclude that she is a traitor,> Ax said.

"Which explains the disguise," I agreed. "But she'd still need access to a Yeerk pool. To Kandrona rays. Which Visser Three wouldn't allow if he thought she was a traitor. Obviously. So . . ."

"So somehow she's alive, somehow she's getting Kandrona rays," Rachel said.

"The question is why?" Cassie said.

"Why what?"

"Why is she here, on Earth? Look, we know going way back that Vissers One and Three are enemies. Visser One let us escape from Visser Three early on. Visser Three must have suspected she was behind that. Then he's got the fact that we let her live when we could have finished her off. So he must want her bad. So why is she walking around downtown? I mean, wig or no wig, Earth isn't a safe place for her."

Rachel grinned. "Come on, it's obvious. She's here to take down Visser Three. Why else? It's her only way out. Take down her main enemy. Then get herself straight with whoever is above them both."

I nodded. It made sense. Figure Rachel to understand the mind of Visser One.

"Whatever her exact motives, it's bad news for us," Cassie said.

"Not necessarily," Jake said. "Warring Vissers are a lot easier to handle than Vissers united against us."

<Divide and conquer,> Ax agreed. <We may be able to use the feud between the Vissers to our advantage.>

Jake nodded. "First step, find out what's in that office."

"She's on twenty-two, third door to the right off the elevator," I said.

<We might be able to gain access from the roof,> Ax suggested.

"Tobias?"

<Yeah, I know the Sutherland Tower,> he said. <There's a door on the roof that probably opens on a staircase leading to the top-floor hall. There's a padlock but the door's pretty rickety. We should have no problem getting in.>

31

"Fly morph?" Cassie said. "Up to the roof as a bird, demorph, morph a fly . . ."

"Not recommended. I had a bad experience with the ventilation system today. But a fast, heavier bug would work, one that can go under doors and through walls."

"You mean . . ."

"That's right." I grinned. "Everyone's favorite houseguest. The wily cockroach."

"We do this right away," Jake directed. "Tonight. But I'm out. Family function."

"Me, too," Rachel said, rolling her eyes. "I promised my mother I'd baby-sit for Jordan and Sara. And I have blown my mom off way too much lately."

"I hate to do this," Cassie said, "but I'm out, too. I am one test away from a 'D' in math. If I get a 'D' my parents will be in my life twenty-four hours a day."

<Ax and I are available,> Tobias said. <No families, no homes, nothing to do but watch the owls eat my mice. Ax-man and I will handle this.>

"And me, obviously," I said.

Jake looked at me.

"What about your dad?" Cassie asked quickly. She was trying to give me an out.

"What about him? He's been working twelve-hour days on a big project. He comes home, he plops on the couch, he watches ESPN. He'll never know I'm gone."

Jake continued to look at me. Rachel looked away.

<There's the problem of Visser One inhabiting your mother's body,> Ax stated bluntly. <And the temptations that seeing her again might arouse.>

Leave it to Ax to be blunt.

"Ax is right, Marco," Cassie said. "Coming face-to-face with Visser One again will be hard for you. And dangerous. For all of us."

"Did I give myself away on the Royan Island mission?" I demanded. "Or today?"

"First time, pretty close," Rachel muttered.

"No, not pretty close," I snapped. "I *didn't*. And that's the fact."

There was an awkward silence.

"I don't believe this crap," I said. "We've been through this before. The mission comes first. Personal hang-ups, second. I'm in. I'm going. Period."

Jake sighed. "Okay, Marco, Ax, and Tobias. Tonight." He looked at me. "Don't do anything foolish. It's reconnaissance only."

I nodded.

"And if it comes to a judgment call, Tobias makes the call."

That caught me off guard. But there was no point arguing. In Jake's place I'd have done the same thing.

"No problem."

Jake came and took my arm and drew me with him outside into the afternoon sunlight. I cringed. I knew what was coming.

"I noticed a certain lack of details about what happened today," Jake said. "Which tells me you did things that I probably don't want to hear about."

"Yeah. You probably don't." I tried out a devil-may-care grin. Not a big success.

Jake folded his arms over his chest and looked down at the ground in silence. Then up at me.

Jake has changed a lot over the months we've been fighting this little war. The look he gave me did not come from my boy Jake, my bud, my pal. It came from a battle commander.

Freaky seeing how old Jake has gotten.

"Marco, you're my best friend. But if you ever go off like that again you and I will have serious problems."

In the old days I'd have said "Bite me," or something equally brilliant.

Now I said, "Okay, understood."

It was all I could do to stop myself from saying, "Yes, sir."

CHAPTER 7

At eleven-thirty that night, with my dad safely snoring in his room, I morphed to seagull and flew to one of the little urban parks scattered throughout the downtown area. Benches, shrubs, trash cans, a few spindly trees. A place where the suits go to eat their bagel sandwiches.

I landed on the dusty ground to pick through the bounty that is an overturned garbage can when I heard the call of a bird of prey. Reluctantly I turned away from the remains of a gyro and took off to join a red-tailed hawk coming in from the north and a northern harrier, coming from the south.

A scavenger like the seagull are good flyers, low and fast. But not nearly as good as hawks and harriers. Too fat from gorging on hot dogs and clams, maybe. By the time I joined Ax and Tobias on the roof of the Sutherland Tower, I was exhausted from pushing for all that altitude.

<The light's not on in the office,> Tobias said.

<She's there,> I said confidently. She had to be. <Let's try that door.>

The door Tobias had told us about earlier wasn't keeping anyone out, least of all a roach. Clearly at one point someone had pried his way in with a crowbar, leaving gouges plenty wide for even a hefty seagull.

But roach was the way to go.

They say that after the big one, total nuclear annihilation, when every other living thing has been turned into a pile of glowing mud, roaches will still be powering over the ruins of civilization.

The amazing indestructible roach. They adapt almost immediately to whatever poison is unleashed on them. And they eat virtually anything — books, glue, plants, dead fish, old sneakers. It's almost impossible to destroy them.

I like that about cockroaches.

The wind was whipping. Heavy clouds covered the moon and the stars. Only the lights on in the surrounding buildings pierced the gloom. We were three mutants on a depressing, deserted island in the sky. An acre of tarred gravel and air-conditioning machinery surrounded us. There was a flagpole, no flag. The hoist kept slapping the pole with a sort of hollow twang.

The sight of Ax halfway between Andalite and cockroach was more interesting than disturbing. Like an armadillo from planet Kill-or-Be-Killed. A cat-sized beetle with a shell made of steel and six roach legs, each with an Andalite hoof. Add to that a foot-long tail with a spike made to stab and you have one mean-looking being.

Tobias, on the other hand, looked disgusting.

Red-tailed hawks and cockroaches were not meant to merge. You've got absolute majesty on the one hand and absolute utility on the other. Mother Nature didn't come up with a birdbug on her own for good reason.

Tobias's beak had transformed into a jaw, opening and shutting involuntarily. Pencil-size antennae jutted from his head. Two hairy stumps poked from the sides of his hawk neck. His wings had molted and shifted onto his back. I watched as they hardened into translucent shell. Below them I could see roach wings growing out of the top of his head.

I shuddered and started my own morph. Focused on all that was roach. Garbage, dark corners, bathrooms, opened cereal boxes . . .

My skin hardened first, scalp to toes.

My arms fused to my sides, then migrated to my back.

Four legs crept out of my sides and I fell forward. The floor had already been getting closer and closer as I shrank to the size of a quarter.

My vision pixilated. Compound roach eyes, with about two thousand lenses, were in place.

My antennae twitched as the roach's amazing sense of smell surged to life. Roaches can smell everything. Good smells like bacon frying. Bad smells like dog poop.

The roof smelled like tar and electricity and cigarette butts.

My innards lost definition and became one long intestinal tract. My mouth lost its lips. My tongue gravitated back into my throat and became a crop, a kind of second mouth.

And then the roach brain turned on. I was in the open.

Way open.

No shelter! No protection!

Fear! Fear! Fear!

I charged ahead and narrowly missed ramming another cockroach. I turned, scrambled across the tar paving of the roof, skittered across a pile of broken glass, and launched. I did an Evel Knievel into Ax.

<Marco, Tobias, I believe you may be in the grip of the cockroach instincts,> Ax said.

<Oh, and you're not?> Tobias countered. <I see you: You're six inches up the flagpole!>

<Okay, okay, everyone stop,> I said. <Nobody move. Where are we heading?>

<The door. Which is . . . well . . .>

Ten minutes later we found our way back to the door. We crept through the ravaged door and skittered wildly down the steps.

There are two ways a roach can go down a set of stairs. It can climb across each tread and down each riser, or it can simply leap off each step and land on the step below.

Unfortunately, we had a lot of steps to go to get down to the twenty-second floor.

So I suggested a third possibility.

39

CHAPTER 8

<The railing is continuous,> I pointed out. <We could race down along the railing.>

<What if we fall off?> Tobias asked.

<We land on the steps, big deal,> I said.

<What if we fall off to the right?>

I was afraid he was going to bring that up. Roach eyes couldn't see that far but I was pretty sure it was a straight drop all the way down. <Then we find out just how far a roach can fall without getting killed.>

<We do have to watch our time in morph,> Tobias said.

The railing was cylindrical painted steel. A bar welded here and there, but basically snaking downward in a long, steep series of tight ovals.

40

Climbing it was hard. Even for a roach. The paint was slick. Fortunately, it had been painted many times and the cracks and runs of many paint jobs gave us footholds.

Still, it was like climbing the Washington Monument. At the top we scrambled over onto the railing itself.

Picture one of those Olympic ski jumps. Only you can't see well enough to see the end. And it's curved, so you can slide off left or right. And if it's right you are going to fall for about three days.

I was in the lead.

<I think we just go for it,> I said. <I mean, all out instead of creeping along.>

<Twenty floors,> Tobias said. <Two turns equal a floor. Forty turns.>

<I will keep track,> Ax offered.

Ax has no faith in our human ability to do simple things like count. With good reason.

<The horses are at the starting gate,> I said. <And . . . they're off!>

I motored my roach legs and rocketed down the railing.

<Aaaaahhhhhh!>

Zooooooom!

Down the railing!

You think a roach looks fast from five feet up as you're trying to stomp it on the kitchen floor? It looks a lot faster down at roach level.

My face was a millimeter off the "ground." Like being strapped facedown underneath someone's Porsche.

My legs were splayed too wide, so that with each of my steps, each of my six legs slipped off into the air. The result was a sort of lurching, out-of-control run that had me skinning along on my belly half the time.

<Aaaahhhhh!> Tobias yelled from behind me.

<First turn!> I yelled.

I hit the turn going at what felt like two hundred miles an hour. I slid to my right to catch the banked corner.

It was total toboggan. It was the luge with rockets strapped to your butt. It was a ride that a skateboarder would have traded his kidneys for.

Down at insane speed, feet motoring, slipping, belly skinning, antennae whipping back. The "road" was a balance beam that had been replaced by a pipe.

It was insane!

<Turn!>

I whipped into a second turn, and now my momentum had taken over. There was no stopping. There was no slowing down. We were out of control. We were projectiles, barely making contact with the steel, banking into 5g turns that would have dropped our guts out through our toes. If we'd had guts. Or toes.

Floor after floor! Bare escape after bare escape. Skittering, scrabbling, fighting, running like someone who's being dragged behind a bus.

<Two more turns and we are there,> Ax yelled.

<What do we do?>

<Jump!>

<Jump? When?>

<NOW!> Ax yelled.

CHAPTER 9

I went into the final turn. No banking this time. It was time for the sled to go off the path while the announcer said, "Oh! Ladies and gentlemen, there's been a terrible accident; I hope everyone's okay!"

I hit the turn. I did not drop down to take the turn. I kept motoring, straight ahead. Straight ahead and suddenly my little roach feet were motoring on air.

<Aaaaahhhhh!>

I fell.

I fell a long way.

Plop!

I hit the floor.

Plop! Plop!

Ax and Tobias landed nearby.

<You okay?>

<Yeah. Ax-man?>

<I am fine.>

<That was cool!> I said.

<Way cool!> Tobias agreed.

<Let's never, *ever* do that again!> I said.

<Never. Ever.>

<Repetition of that activity would be a very bad idea,> Ax agreed.

We scooted over to, then under a fire door, with the steel scraping our backs, and into the hallway of the twenty-second floor.

The hall was dark except for a weak ray of light from the bottom of a closed door just ahead. We raced along the industrial carpet, hugging the wall.

Then the door to the lighted office opened.

A man stepped out and the hall lights went on.

Panic!

<Nobody move!>

We stood stock-still as the looming figure took another step.

"IRS and their audits," the man muttered.

He turned the lights off and locked the door behind him. Then he went ballistic.

"Roach!" he cried. I felt the violent vibration of his massive human foot slam down on the carpet.

<Ax! Tobias!>

<I am right behind you, Marco,> Ax replied.

<I think he got a *real* roach,> Tobias said. <Just stay put. Freeze!>

The man walked toward the elevator, muttering about how much rent he was paying for his office and there were roaches and they said it was a luxury building, hah!

There was a DING announcing the elevator's arrival. The hall lights went off. The elevator door closed. We were alone on the twenty-second floor.

Except, of course, for my mom.

No, not my mom, I told myself. I couldn't start thinking that way.

She was Visser One. That's who we were up against.

We scurried on until we reached what I was pretty sure was the door to the Visser's office. Up along the doorjamb, then across the surface of the door to the base of the window set in the center.

The roach's vision was not so spectacular. Still, I could make out enough of the room to decide it looked like a normal office. A reception desk, a plush chair, a leather couch, phones, computer, printer, a copy machine, a coffee-maker.

Nothing Yeerk about it at all.

<Perhaps we have the wrong location,> Ax said.

<I know I saw her go in here this morning.>

<We've got to go in. I didn't just survive the roller coaster from hell to turn around and give up.> Tobias said as he led the way. We skittered back down the door and tried to squeeze under it. No luck.

<An impenetrable seal,> Ax noted. <Probably around the entire doorframe.>

<No one puts this tight a seal around an average office door.> I sighed. <Looks like the air vent's our best bet.>

I led the way up the wall and through the air vent I'd been sucked into that morning.

<Which way?> Tobias asked.

<I'm guessing to the right.>

We scrambled through scatterings of lint and ash to a vent that opened into what had to be the Visser's lair. Assuming the Visser was preparing to go to war with a small country.

<Hologram paint,> Ax explained. <One can paint a window, project a hologram onto the back of this paint, and thereby disguise a room. The Visser has projected the picture of a normal office onto the back of the paint. Very clever.>

<So anyone who passes by, like a security guard, won't know what's going down in here,> Tobias added.

<It's got to be on the exterior windows, too,> I surmised. <To fool window washers.>

<Or red-tailed hawks. Let's do this quick and get out of here.>

In almost total darkness we crawled out through the grate and along the ceiling until we reached a wall. Then down the wall and onto the gray industrial carpeting.

<I'll demorph first,> Ax said. <In case there is need for defense.>

In a few minutes, we were in our normal forms. With our keen Andalite, hawk, and human senses.

It was then I wished I was still a roach. A roach would not have seen so clearly what I saw now.

In the corner of the room was a small, portable Yeerk pool. Like a stainless-steel Jacuzzi. The steel-bound briefcase I'd seen that morning was nearby.

On the lip of the portable Yeerk pool was a large clamp. A sort of collar.

My mother's neck was in that collar. It held her tight. It held her head sideways, so that one side of her face, one ear, was pressed into the water.

The rest of her body stood awkwardly, help-lessly, bent over.

<The Yeerk is feeding,> Ax said coldly.

A Yeerk must return to the Yeerk pool every three days to absorb Kandrona rays. Otherwise it starves.

The complex box was a portable Kandrona.

My mother was, for this time, for just these few moments, my mother. The Yeerk slug that was Visser One was out of her head, in the liquid, feeding.

Right now she was my mom.

Five steps and I would be beside her.

I moved.

CHAPTER 10

<Marco!> Tobias snapped.

A second step. A third!

<Ax!>

Suddenly there was an Andalite tail blade at my throat.

I stopped.

<No, Marco,> Ax said calmly. <Visser One will be back in your mother's head the second she senses any danger. And you could not open those locks with force. They are no doubt controlled by a brain-wave interface. So that the Yeerk can maintain control, even outside your mother's body.>

I grabbed his tail and tried to shove it away.

But an Andalite tail is nothing but one long, coiled muscle. It moved about three inches.

<Marco, stop it!> Tobias said. <Back off and think about it! Right now she's turned away, so she can't see you. You step into her line of sight, she'll *know*.>

I stopped trying to push Ax's tail away.

<We're here to investigate, Marco,> Tobias said gently. <Not the time, my friend. No matter how much you want it to be, this isn't the time.>

<What if you fail, Marco?> Ax asked. <If you reveal yourself but are unable to stop the Yeerk from reentering her. What then, Marco?>

My mother was locked into a vise, three feet away from me. Maybe Ax was wrong. Maybe I could release the clamp. Maybe . . .

I stepped back.

I felt like dirt. She was right there! Free, if only for a moment. I could tell her I was okay! I could tell her . . .

Nothing. I could tell her nothing. Ax was probably right. I would not have been able to free her. Visser One would reinfest. Security would be breached. Our secret revealed. And then?

And then we would have to destroy the innocent as well as the guilty.

It made sense. It was the cold, calculated, smart thing to do.

I wiped my hand over my face. It came away wet.

"What's that? In the corner," I whispered, distracting myself.

<Surveillance and communications equipment.>

It was a console about the size of an upright piano. On top sat a satellite dish, pointed toward the outside window. In the middle of the console was a large screen. And on that screen were images that seemed to have been shot from above.

Images that were disturbingly familiar. Images of free Hork-Bajir.

<Visser One knows about the Hork-Bajir colony,> Tobias said grimly. <That's what she's up to.>

<Handheld Dracon weapons over there, surveillance devices, a portable Yeerk pool,> Ax observed, looking around the room with his stalk eyes. <Everything the Visser needs for guerrilla action.>

<That briefcase, by the side of the Yeerk pool,> Tobias said. <Is that what she was carrying this morning, Marco?>

"Yeah. And there's another one on the desk by the window," I whispered.

<Emergency Kandrona Particle Generators,> Ax surmised. <One use each. It appears the Vis-

ser only has six days to finish whatever it is she's started.>

"Rot in hell!"

It was said softly, but ferociously. We froze.

My mother's voice! But who was she talking to? To us? Did she know we were there? Had she heard us?

No. No, of course: She was talking to the Yeerk. It must have begun to reinfest her.

BBWWBBWWBBWW!

The room started to tremble. I jumped, startled out of my trance.

<What?> Tobias demanded.

"Out of here!" I hissed.

We darted through a second door. Into a small, private bathroom.

BAM!

Even in the bathroom I felt the shock of the blow. Someone or something slamming the office door with the force of a battering ram.

BAM! BAM!

"The Yeerks," I said. "They're here to kill her!"

<Then they will be doing our job for us,> Ax answered coldly.

"Not while I stand around and watch," I said.

<The person in the next room is not your mother. It is Visser One. She will kill you the first chance she gets.>

I ignored him. Gorilla. It was my favorite power morph and I was ready to bust some heads. If I couldn't save my mother from her Yeerk, at least I could save her from whoever was trying to kill Visser One.

<You are being extremely foolish,> Ax said.

"Bull. You're letting your hatred of Yeerks get in the way. If Visser Three is trying to kill Visser One there may be an opening for us."

<An opportunity?> Tobias said thoughtfully.

<Maybe,> Ax allowed. <But Prince Jake said we were not to —>

"Blame me," I muttered.

<We will,> Tobias said with a laugh.

FWAM!

The outer door crashed in.

TSEEEW! TSEEEW!

The familiar sounds of Dracon beams firing!

I opened the bathroom door. In the office, total chaos.

The Visser had freed my mother's body from the pool and she was crouched behind the surveillance console. She was firing a Dracon beam.

A Hork-Bajir was staggering back, a burning hole in its chest. But more were pushing through the doorway.

<Party time,> I said, now fully gorilla.

I opened the bathroom door and barreled out.

Visser One shot a surprised glance at me. She hesitated. Should she shoot?

Two huge Hork-Bajir rushed her. She turned her attention back to them. Too late!

A bladed arm swung. It was meant to remove my mother's arm. It missed and knocked the weapon from her hand.

She was helpless. The Hork-Bajir leaned close.

WHUMPF!

My fist flattened the snout of the Hork-Bajir. He staggered back. Visser One dived for her Dracon beam. Ax leaped from the bathroom.

"Andalite!" one of the Hork-Bajir yelled in shock.

FWAPP!

Ax's tail blade did to the Hork-Bajir what he'd intended doing to my mom.

But the Hork-Bajir were still coming. There were four in the room. More outside.

"Tseeeeer!"

Tobias flapped, talons out. A flurry of russet feathers and the Hork-Bajir fell back, clutching his eyes.

We fought our way through the stunned aliens, smashing and slashing. And then, out of the corner of my eye, I saw Visser One level her Dracon beam. At *me*!

Too far away for me to reach her. <Ax!> I yelled.

FWAPP!

The bullwhip-fast tail slammed the portable Kandrona and knocked it into her head.

<Rather stupid, Visser, since we are attempting to save your life,> he said to her.

"I don't take help from Andalites!" she screamed in rage. But her weapon was out of reach. Hork-Bajir blocked any hope of retrieving it.

The Visser turned and ran into the bathroom.

I jumped to my feet, just in time, for an injured Hork-Bajir flailing blindly was about to cut a deep gash in my side. I grabbed it by one of its bladed arms and flung it into a wall. I sunk my fist into a second Hork-Bajir. And Tobias did his own damage. But it was Ax who was winning this fight. His tail was whipping left, right, too fast for the eye to follow.

The Hork-Bajir fell back before him. Fell back fighting at first, then in panic. They fought to get back out through the door.

I grabbed the splintered mess of door and shoved it back in place.

I gave Ax a look. <Dude. I think you really scared them.>

<We obviously took them by surprise,> he said modestly.

<I hear chopper blades,> Tobias said, hawk head cocked.

<Is it a getaway, or reinforcements?>

<Don't know. Marco. Open that window for me.>

I picked up a chair and threw it against the window. It shattered. <In high-rise office buildings the windows don't open,> I said.

Tobias flew out through shards of glittering glass. He reported immediately. <They're outta here!>

"Die, Andalite!"

The bathroom door flew open. An arm was raised. A frail-looking arm. With a not-at-all-frail-looking Dracon beam.

She'd stashed a weapon in the bathroom!

TSEEEW! TSEEEW!

The light beams were aimed dead-center at Ax. But Ax wasn't there by the time she'd pulled the trigger.

I dove for the floor and shot forward, sliding on spilt Hork-Bajir blood. The Visser was crouched behind the surveillance console again, hate in her eyes. In my massive fist I grabbed one of the Visser's enormous briefcases and blocked a shot aimed at my head.

With all the power of my gorilla muscles and all the rage of a kid bent on revenge, I leaped forward, tumbled over the surveillance console, and onto Visser One.

WHHUMMPPFFF.

Four hundred pounds of muscle and flesh crushing my mother's slim human body.

I stood up, yanked her to her feet, calmly disarmed her, and tossed the weapon aside. I put her in an armlock.

A gentle armlock.

<We save your regrettable life and you try to kill us,> Ax sneered. <You are a perfect representative of your species.>

"So why don't you kill me?" Visser One spat. "Arrogant Andalite filth! Why don't you kill me now?"

<As you wish,> Ax said, nodding to me. <For my part I say: Kill her.>

CHAPTER 11

<Kill her now,> Ax said in public thought-speak.

But in a private aside, heard only by me and Tobias, he added, <I am speaking only for dramatic effect, of course. But it would be good for the Yeerk to be frightened.>

I tightened my grip. Let her feel the irresistible power in my arms. I resisted the urge to cry, "I'm sorry, Mom!"

"Stop!" the Visser screamed. "Don't kill me!"

I relaxed my massive arms. My mother's human body slumped. I could hear her labored breathing. See her shoulder blades through the thin silk blouse she wore.

<Why shouldn't we kill you?> Ax taunted. <You Yeerks killed my brother, Elfangor.>

"Elfangor's brother! I might have known some branch of his squalid, cowardly family still lived! But it was Visser Three who ended Elfangor's evil life. He's the one you want. And so do I. I want him dead as much as you do. Not that I wouldn't have been proud to claim Elfangor as my own victim."

<I'm going to let her go,> I said. I couldn't hold her any longer. I was halfway between a loving hug and a furious strangle.

<She may still have concealed weapons,> Ax said privately.

<Hey, I am not frisking my own mother.>

<She's not carrying anything,> Tobias said. <I'd see it.>

I let her go. She straightened her blonde wig and took a few deep breaths.

I knocked the wig from her head with a sudden backhand. I don't know why.

The Visser . . . my mother . . . shot me a look of cold amusement. "Gentle Andalite warrior," she said mockingly.

<You're alive. So be quiet,> I snapped.

"I won't be alive for long," she said, suddenly weary. "Visser Three had accused me of treason. Now, once his Hork-Bajir report, he'll have the proof he can take to the Council of Thirteen.

They've issued a *gashad*. A warrant to kill me on sight."

Tobias flew over to the photographs we'd seen earlier. <What were you up to?>

She laughed. "And wouldn't you like to know its every detail."

<Yes, we would,> Ax said. <And you will tell us. Or you will die.>

"I'm already dead."

<Your plan must involve discrediting Visser Three,> Ax said. <We might help. If it were Visser Three with the *gashad* on his head, your own head would be more secure.>

Her dark eyes glittered. "You help me destroy Visser Three, then you destroy me. Is that the plan?"

<Yes,> I said bluntly.

She laughed derisively. "The truth. You do me the honor of not taking me for a fool."

<And if you get the chance you will destroy Visser Three, and then us,> I said.

She leaned close, bringing her face so close to mine. "Yes, I will."

<Now, Yeerk,> Ax said, <you will tell us your story. I would advise hurrying. Visser Three's forces will be back.>

I watched as my mother's body straightened. Her voice was calm, unemotional.

"I had returned to Earth to construct an un-

61

derwater facility. It would produce a host body useful for the invasion of Leera. But, as you Andalites know, that facility was destroyed. I was disgraced. I was demoted to sub-Visser rank. But Visser Three set out to complete my destruction. He told anyone who would listen that I was a traitor. The Council of Thirteen believed him and issued the *gashad*. I have been in hiding ever since."

<Yet, here you are, on Earth. Seemingly alone,> Ax said. <No doubt there is a ship in orbit. And perhaps a Bug fighter hidden here on the planet. No doubt you have more of the emergency Kandrona generators on board.>

The Visser shook her head. "I'm not leading you to my ship, Andalite."

Before I knew what I was doing, before I had time to think, I snatched up the portable Kandrona and slammed it hard on the floor.

<Tell her "ticktock," Ax,> I said.

"A good tactical move," the Visser said. "Shorten my time. Make me desperate. But it won't work."

<We'll see,> I muttered.

<What is your plan, Yeerk?> Ax pressed. <What information do you have on Visser Three that could redeem you in the eyes of the Council of Thirteen?>

Visser One relaxed my mother's body against the shot-up surveillance console. For a moment she looked as innocent as a third-grade teacher about to tell a folksy story about the young Abe Lincoln.

"Free Hork-Bajir," she said simply. "Visser Three has allowed escaped Hork-Bajir to start a colony right under his nose."

<But the Yeerks have enslaved the entire Hork-Bajir population,> Ax replied. <There are no free Hork-Bajir left in the galaxy, much less here on Earth.>

"Don't play dumb with me," the Visser said. "It's the one thing we admire about you Andalites: your intelligence."

<Where did you get this theory of yours?> Ax demanded.

"That's my business." Visser One shrugged. "There are all sorts of ways to figure out what is going on underground if you have the mental acuity, which Visser Three most assuredly does not. Tell me Andalite," the Visser continued. "How did your brother, the mighty Elfangor, succumb to so flawed and incompetent a Yeerk as Visser Three?>

<I could ask you the same thing,> Ax replied, calmly.

"I know the importance of revenge to the

Andalite culture," Visser One said. "Visser Three killed your brother. You are honor-bound to kill him. I can make that happen."

<For a price,> Ax said.

"For a price," she agreed.

<What price?> I asked.

"The Hork-Bajir colony. Give me the free Hork-Bajir. I will give you Visser Three."

CHAPTER 12

A moment of silence.

<Tell her we agree,> I told Ax privately.

Tobias erupted. <Are you insane! There's no way we're giving up the Hork-Bajir!>

<No, we won't. But she doesn't know that. She thinks we're Andalites. You know the one word Yeerks always use in describing Andalites? Ruthless. That's what they think. She'll buy it.>

Ax said, <That is all you ask, Yeerk? The free Hork-Bajir?> He laughed. <I was concerned you might demand something of value.>

"We have a deal?"

Ax said, <Tobias?>

65

<You had so better know what you're doing, Marco my man,> Tobias said to me. <This is way beyond anything Jake and the others have approved. We're doing a deal with the enemy.>

<You want Visser Three?> I shot back. <She can give us Visser Three.>

<And then she replaces him,> Tobias said. <I know Ax's motive here: He has a personal score with Visser Three. The question is, do you have a personal problem here as well?>

<It's good strategy, Tobias. You know I'm good at that. You know I'm good at seeing the main chance.>

<Yeah. You are. But that's your mother.>

I couldn't argue with that. <Jake left it up to you, Tobias.>

Tobias laughed without any humor. <You'd better not be playing us, Marco. If it comes down to it, Visser One . . . no matter what host body . . . is meat. You know that, right? You're clear on that.>

<I'm clear,> I said.

<Okay, Ax-man,> Tobias said.

<We have a deal,> Ax said.

"Tell me where to find the free Hork-Bajir!"

<You will be given that information when the time comes,> Ax said. <Once Visser Three is exposed, I will kill him. That way, you will have not

committed treason by murdering a full Visser and I will have achieved my sworn revenge.>

"One more thing: You and the rest of your gang will be there. I will need you to help me eliminate the free Hork-Bajir. I am one person, all alone."

Ax started to answer. I stopped him.

<Agree, Ax.>

<What?> Tobias demanded.

<Alone my butt,> I said. <She has some kind of force. She's too calm. Too relaxed about Visser Three trying another attack here. She already has her forces nearby. Agree to what she asks.>

<A Hork-Bajir is a Hork-Bajir,> Ax said indifferently. <No more than animals to us.>

"Contact me when you are ready," she said.

<How?>

She smiled then. A smile that was my mother's smile. Again I felt the opposite urges: to cry and to destroy.

"I have E-mail." She laughed and told us the address.

Then she narrowed her eyes and looked at us, each, one after the other. "One of you does almost all the talking. Two of you stay in morph. Visser Three is a fool. He has overlooked something strange about your group of rebels. He has missed something."

She grinned a savage grin. "But don't worry. When I am returned to power I will figure it out. And then . . ." She made a gun hand, pointed it at my head, and said, "and then . . . TSEEEEW!"

CHAPTER 13

We left. We demorphed in the stairwell and climbed the stairs the hard way. As soon as we reached the roof Tobias took to the air to catch a look around.

<Four helicopters on the way,> he reported. <They'll be here in five minutes. Visser One will have a bunch of Visser Three's Hork-Bajir down on her before she knows it.>

"Let's get wings," I suggested to Ax.

Moments later we all three took to the air. It was hard flying. No updrafts, no thermals at night, just dead air you have to flap your way through like a bat.

We flew through the tall concrete and steel forest. Here and there a single light, or the lights

69

of an entire floor burned. I saw cleaning people pushing wheeled trash cans and vacuums.

One light illuminated a room full of tired-looking men and women eating pizza and standing around some kind of chart.

It's strange, but flying near tall buildings always makes you feel like you're higher up. You notice the altitude, I guess, when you realize you're flying past the fortieth floor or whatever.

No one said anything till we were clear. The clatter of helicopters was loud behind us.

I was confident that Visser Three's troops would find an empty room.

<Well, Marco, you've just agreed to betray Jara Hamee, Toby, the entire Hork-Bajir colony. You'd better have a plan.>

<I do.>

<Gonna tell us about it?>

<We're going to take them both down. Vissers One and Three,> I said. <They want to kill each other, we'll help them.>

I could sense Tobias's hesitation. <You're setting up your mom?>

<No. I'm setting up Visser One.>

<Marco, she's —>

<Shut up, Tobias,> I snapped. <Okay? I know all about it. You guys don't think I'll do it? Well,

here's a news flash: I'll do it. Me. Not any of you. Me. My plan, okay?>

<You don't have to prove anything, dude,> Tobias said.

<It's not about proving anything. It's about winning this stupid war.>

<We must speak with Prince Jake, of course. Inform him of what we have learned. Obtain his approval of your plan.> Ax, of course.

<It's the middle of the night. We can't get to Jake right now. Not with Tom home. We'll talk to Jake tomorrow. Right now, we act.>

Tobias shifted his wings, moving slightly away. I swear, I've never met anyone who could express disapproval the way Tobias can.

But at that moment I didn't care what Tobias thought. Taking control, doing, would keep me from dwelling on it. From falling apart.

I knew Tobias and Ax were doubtful. I knew they didn't entirely trust me. They thought I was playing a double game. But they were wrong. I had seen the way to destroy both Vissers. I had seen it in all its perfection.

People don't understand the word *ruthless.* They think it means "mean." It's not about being mean. It's about seeing the bright, clear line that leads from A to B. The line that goes from motive to means. Beginning to end.

It's about seeing that bright, clear line and not caring about anything but the beautiful fact that you can see the solution. Not caring about anything else but the perfection of it.

That's what had happened. I saw the way to take both Vissers down. And that's all that mattered.

But I wasn't going to explain all that. Other people's pity just messes with the straight line. Other people's pity makes you think things you can't think about when you are seeing the line.

<Look, we're gonna need to acquire an animal native to mountaintops. But I'm not a zoologist, so we go see Cassie.>

<It's the middle of the night where Cassie lives, too,> Tobias said.

<Yeah, but she doesn't have a Controller in the house with her,> I said.

<We do not know that for certain,> Ax pointed out.

<If you guys want to bail, fine. I can do this alone.>

A bluff. I knew they'd hang with me. Tobias had no choice. He could either try and stop me forcefully, or go along.

<You're a jerk, Marco,> Tobias said.

<Yeah, I love you, too,> I said.

CHAPTER 14

The night was peaceful as we flew.

I knew in my heart that four chopper loads of Hork-Bajir had burst into an empty office and found no one. Knew it. I don't believe in destiny. But I felt destiny this time.

We would meet, Visser One and I. We would meet on a mountaintop. And I would end it all there.

Only a few stars shone high in the sky through the thinning clouds. We flew closer together than we ordinarily would during the day, when the sight of three birds of prey grouped together in the sky would attract unwanted attention. We flew from downtown to uptown, across the neighborhood where Jake and I and Rachel live, out

73

past more suburbs, and into the almost country where Cassie's family has their home and the Wildlife Rehabilitation Center.

We landed in a large, leafy tree whose branches gently scraped Cassie's bedroom window. Tobias moved close, walking the comical sideways bird walk, like a parrot in its cage. He tapped on the window with his beak.

TAP. TAP. TAP.

<She's not moving,> he said.

<Is she in there?> I asked.

<No, it's after midnight, so naturally she's out in the yard playing Hacky Sack,> Tobias snipped.

He was ticked at having control taken from him.

<Hacky Sack?> I said.

<Hacky Sack?> Ax echoed.

<Everyone shut up!> Tobias said in exasperation.

<Tap louder.>

<Gee, do you think, Marco?>

TAP! TAP! TAP!

<Nothing. Must be dreaming about . . .>

TAP! TAP! TA-CSSSHHHH!

The glass shattered. It fell in a shower of glittering shards.

<Oops.>

"Jake?" Cassie bolted upright in bed.

<Awww, isn't that sweet?> I said, so Cassie

74

could hear. <Her first thought is "Jake." Makes you wonder just what kind of dreams she was having.>

<Cassie, it's us,> Tobias said. <Sorry about the glass.>

"I'm going to have to explain this you know," Cassie said, rubbing the sleep out of her eyes. Then, belatedly, she snatched modestly at the neck of her sleep shirt.

<Just say a bird hit the window,> Ax suggested. <You would not be lying.>

"That would be a change from routine," Cassie muttered. "What are you guys doing?"

<Checking out babes,> I suggested.

"Marco, what are you all doing here? What happened tonight? Is anyone hurt?"

<We are unhurt,> Ax said.

<We need a good morph for traveling in the mountains,> I said. <Something that can climb. Something with some size, if possible. Some ability to inflict punishment.>

"You better not have woken me up and broken my window to —"

<Kind of a ticktock situation, here —> I interrupted.

Cassie looked doubtfully at Tobias, then Ax.

<Marco has a plan,> Tobias said dryly.

"Jake?"

<Cassie, just help us, okay?> I said.

She sucked in a deep breath. "Okay. Mountain goat."

<Good! A goat from The Gardens' petting zoo. What could be easier to acquire?>

"Not that kind of goat, Marco." Cassie shook her head. "A mountain goat. Sharp horns. Amazing agility. A hind-leg kick that could send a person through a barn wall. Those guys can weigh almost three hundred pounds."

<Fine, fine,> I said. <Where do we get one?>

Cassie hesitated. "Is he okay?" she asked Tobias, referring to me.

<Seems to be.>

"Tobias, this is a stressful situation for Marco. Jake put you in charge. If Marco is —"

<Hey! Hey! Am I invisible? I'm here, okay?>

"Okay, then. I'll ask *you*. Are you okay, Marco? You seem kind of jazzed. Manic."

I said a harsh word. Then, <Everyone stop acting like I'm some kind of dimwit. I know what I'm doing. I don't need a bunch of psychoanalysis, here. This isn't *Oprah*!>

Cassie bit her lip thoughtfully. She got a distracted look in her eyes. I realized she was listening to Tobias or Ax or both communicating in private thought-speak. I don't know what they told her. But I saw that flicker of emotion in her eyes: pity.

"Well," she said at last, "The Gardens has a

newish mountainside habitat. It's open-air so you shouldn't have any trouble getting in after hours. Or getting near the goats."

I launched from the windowsill. Neither Ax nor Tobias spoke to me as we traveled. Maybe they were privately ripping me apart. I didn't care.

I saw the bright, clear line.

CHAPTER 15

The Gardens: Kick-butt amusement park meets zoo. Very expensive admission price. If you go in through the gate.

I spotted the darkened Ferris wheel ahead, and my favorite, the snaking, sloping roller coaster in the amusement park section of The Gardens. A moment later, flying over the zoo, I saw what had to be the mountainside habitat Cassie'd told us about.

A rolling, grassy plain. A stream meandering across the north end. And in the middle of the plain, an imposing, incredibly steep stone and concrete "mountain" full of shallow caves and terraces. The habitat itself was surrounded by a high mesh fence, on top of which we landed.

I could make out the dim, humped shapes of several goats just inside the largest of the shallow caves. They were sitting on the ground in a cluster. Several more goats stood motionless, staring back at the three large birds staring at them.

<Interesting,> Ax observed. <Bearded, white-coated creatures with hooves. And horns. Grazers. I would point out the similarities between the mountain goat and Andalites, except for my extremely disappointing experience with the cow.>

<I think mountain goats might be a bit more intelligent than cattle, Ax,> I said. <And a bit more aggressive. These guys look like they mean business.>

<Look at the shoulders on that one staring at me,> Tobias said nervously. <He's like a line-backer or something.>

<Yes, acquiring one might be quite a challenge,> Ax observed. <Perhaps we should choose one that is asleep.>

<Good idea.> I lifted off and flew to a ledge outside a small cave. Tobias and Ax followed. I'd seen one large shape inside. Yup. A big mountain goat, asleep. Male? I couldn't tell. All of the

goats had black horns and beards though I figured some had to be female.

Ax and I demorphed quietly a few feet away. The fake mountain hadn't looked like all that much when we were birds. As a human, though, the ground looked a long way down.

I swayed and grabbed some rock.

Then I began to crawl over toward the massive, shaggy white beast.

"What if he wakes up?" I said.

<This is your little picnic, you tell me,> Tobias sniped.

I sighed. "Tobias, look, get up off my back, okay? I know you're thinking Jake will blame you if this all goes bad. But we need to just get along, here, okay?"

Tobias laughed. <Okay. I'm done pouting. Unless we end up getting kicked cross-country by these big goats. Then I'll pout plenty.>

I stepped closer. Dumb to be scared of a goat. All the animals I'd been near. All the animals I'd *been*, and I was worried by a goat?

I placed my hand on its side. It looked at me.

"Please don't shove your horns into my kidneys," I said pleasantly.

It stirred. I wanted to pull back. But that would have been the wrong move.

My hand touched rough fur. I focused. I needed to begin acquiring this big boy right now.

The goat seemed about ready to spring up and butt me into the next dimension. But then it settled down as the acquiring trance took hold.

Ax clopped forward and when I withdrew my hand, he laid his own on the goat. Tobias was last.

<Come on, you guys,> he said when he'd hopped off the back of the sleeping goat. <Morph and let's get out of here before it wakes up.>

"Uh, don't look now but I think we have another problem."

On the ledge stood Mr. Mountain Goat's homeboys. And they didn't look happy to see us.

"Uh-oh," I said.

It took the goats approximately two seconds to cover about a hundred feet of ledges, boulders, gullies, and curves.

I turned.

I ran.

Tobias fluttered away to safety. Ax leaped nimbly away. Me? I got goat horn in the butt.

I flew.

"Aaahhhhh!"

Later, I read that male mountain goats enjoy

butting each other with their horns — in each other's butts.

And let me just say that unless you have been butted down a fifteen-foot-high cliff by a two-hundred-and-fifty-pound angry male mountain goat, you have not experienced true humiliation.

CHAPTER 16

I lay in my bed, in the dark. Every few minutes I'd check the glowing numbers of the clock. Three fifteen. Three forty-two. Four-oh-nine.

I wanted to sleep. Needed to sleep. Couldn't.

Ever have one of those nights? Where you're exhausted, where you'd pay anything just to fall asleep? But the wheels in your head just keep spinning and spinning and spinning?

Imagined conversations. Me talking, explaining, arguing. Changing the words around, repeating them, rehashing them. Around and around in circles.

Me talking to Jake, an imaginary Jake. Explaining, with perfect logic..

Me talking to my dad in some fictional future, some nonexistent world where things were different and I could at last tell all the secrets I'd guarded with my life.

Me talking to my mom. Raging. Explaining.

Me explaining to my mom, as my *mom*, as my *real mom*, why I had to do it.

Me explaining to my mom as *Visser One*. Laughing, chortling, savoring my victory over her.

This is how I defeated you! I crowed.

This is how I saved you! I explained.

No choice. No choice.

I had to do it, Dad, you understand, right? What else was I going to do? Too much on the line. I had responsibilities. You know how that is, right? And besides, she was already dead to you. You'd already grieved, remember? You spent years just sitting in your chair, staring blankly, your life falling apart . . .

See, Jake? Don't ever doubt me again. I did it, okay? I put the mission first. I saw the big picture. So just don't ever doubt me again, because I did what had to be done. . . .

Mom, what was I supposed to do? I saw all the plays. I saw all the pieces on the chessboard. There was no solution that freed you. There were only solutions that destroyed you. I had to. How else? How else to . . .

Die, you Yeerk piece of crap. Wither and die, and remember with your last, dying thought: It was for her. I killed you for her.

For Jake.

For my dad.

For . . .

Around and around, as the hours ticked away. As exhaustion sank deep into my bones.

Someday, if we won, if humanity survived, we'd be in the history books. Me and Jake and Rachel and Cassie and Tobias and Ax. They'd be household names, like generals from World War II or the Civil War. Patton and Eisenhower, Ulysses Grant and Robert E. Lee.

Kids would study us in school. Bored, probably.

And then the teacher would tell the story of Marco. I'd be a part of history. What I was about to do.

Some kid would laugh. Some kid would say, "Cold, man. That was really cold."

I had to do it, kid. It was a war. It's the whole point, you stupid, smug, smirking little jerk! Don't you get it?

It was the *whole point*. We hurt the innocent in order to stop the evil.

Innocent Hork-Bajir. Innocent Taxxons. Innocent human-Controllers.

How else to stop the Yeerks? How else to win?

No choice, you punk. We did what we had to do.

"Cold, man. The Marco dude? He was just cold."

CHAPTER 17

The next morning we all met at the barn. I was past tired. My butt was sore. My elbows were raw from skinning down the artificial cliff.

Tobias seemed tired, too. Too tired even to tease me about my encounter with the goat. Ax acted as though he'd spent the night snoozing like a baby.

I explained my plan to Jake and the others.

"We take out Visser One. We take out Visser Three. We leave the Yeerks believing they've erased the free Hork-Bajir colony. The free Hork-Bajir end up much safer; the Yeerks end up leaderless."

I avoided looking at Cassie. From Jake there

was just the briefest flicker of sadness. But Jake, too, is addicted to the bright, clear line.

Rachel kept her eyes down, focusing on the dirt-and-hay floor.

Rachel's not stupid. She knew anything she said would just make me mad. And I guess she, like all of them, was putting herself in my shoes. Wondering if she could do it.

"If it works, we have them both," I concluded. "But there's a lot to go wrong. A lot of unforeseen things that —"

Cassie put a hand on my arm. "Marco, you know we'll try to help your mother, in whatever way we can."

"She's only one person." I shrugged off her hand and stood up. "And we're supposed to be saving the world, right?"

It was one of the lines I'd practiced the night before. It sounded more bitter and less cool and calm and in control than I wanted.

"Okay," Jake said.

That was it. Just "okay." He didn't come out with any of the lines I'd put in his mouth in my imaginary conversations.

"So we do it?" I asked.

"Yeah. You call the plays, Marco."

I sucked in a shaky breath. "Okay. Okay. Okay, we want to push the timing. Don't give Visser One time to think about it. Keep her off balance. I know the place. I hiked near there once with my dad. I need someone to contact Erek."

Erek is one of a small group of Chee. They are androids. Pacifists by programming. But working to infiltrate the Yeerk ranks. Spies.

The Chee pass as human by the use of sophisticated holographic projections. They live human lives. Many human lives. They've been on Earth since the time of the pyramids.

<I'm on it,> Tobias volunteered, flying down from his perch in the hayloft.

"Okay. We don't let her see us. We play the arrogant Andalites the whole way. Visser One can't —"

"She's your mother!" Cassie exploded. "She's not 'Visser One.' She's your mother! Is everyone just going to let this happen?"

Jake sent her a cold look. "This is not the time, Cassie."

"When is it going to be the time? When Marco's mind is screwed up forever by this? He's in denial. This is his mother, for God's sake."

Jake said nothing. No one said anything. Cassie's words just hung in the air.

"Go on, Marco," Jake said finally.

"We want her to focus on disliking Andalite arrogance," I said. "She hates Andalites. So, we want her to dwell on that. Maybe it will be enough to keep her from seeing the trap. As soon as we're ready, I'll E-mail her."

"Ax, do you think we can play the roles of arrogant Andalites?" Jake asked.

<It will certainly require good acting skills to imbue the fundamentally humble and dispassionate Andalite character with a taint of arrogance,> he said.

"Yeah. *Humble* is the very first word that comes to mind when I think 'Andalite,'" Rachel said with a drawl.

<I think I should do as much of it as possible,> Tobias suggested. <I spend the most time with Ax. I can do a pretty good "arrogant Andalite.">

<I am very close to taking offense,> Ax huffed.

"Okay, Tobias. But you have to allow time to get to the mountains."

<I'll have a tailwind. And I go "as the bird flies," not on winding mountain roads.>

I went to the computer Cassie and her dad use to keep medical records. "Ax? We need a secure screen name. Something not even the Yeerks could trace back here."

Ax worked at the computer for a few minutes, muttering about primitive human technology. Muttering in a dispassionately humble way, of course.

<You may compose your message.>

I typed. I hit "send." I didn't think about what I was setting in motion.

"Okay. Everyone understands what's what, right?" I asked.

"Yeah."

"Okay. I'm outta here."

I began to morph to osprey. Moments later, I was in the air. Relieved to be away from my friends.

Approximately fifteen minutes later, I landed in a leafy elm tree near the busy corner of Green and Spring Streets.

Tobias sat on a telephone pole across the street, preening his feathers.

<You get Erek?>

<Yeah. He's on it. Think she'll show? Your m —. I mean, Visser One?>

<Yeah. I think she'll show.>

Minutes later she drove up in a rented Audi. She slammed it into a parking space, bullying her way past a family in a Chrysler Town and Country.

She climbed out. The driver of the van yelled something at her. She gave him a look. He decided to drive off.

She wasn't in the disguise, anymore. She looked like my mom again. She was my mom.

The olive skin. The shampoo-commercial black hair. The dark eyes.

<Visser One,> I told myself.

She stood pretending to be fascinated by the wares displayed in the window of the Ace Hardware.

<You're on, Tobias,> I told him. <Remember: arrogant Andalite.>

<Visser One, you will follow my instructions literally and immediately,> Tobias said.

Her head jerked. She looked around. She eyed a blind woman's guide dog suspiciously.

<You will be crossing paths with a human-Controller named Chapman,> Tobias said.

"Chapman!" she mumbled. "One of Visser Three's incompetents. He would turn me in in a second if it meant his advancement through the ranks."

<Exactly the point, Yeerk. You want Visser Three. Surely you understood that we had to attract his attention. We are delivering him. Do not question me again.>

My osprey eyes could see her mouth form a string of foul words. Tobias ignored her.

<Chapman's afternoon run takes him past the human business called Dunkin' Donuts. It is one street to the east. Walk there now. Make sure he sees you. Do not attempt to escape,> Tobias said. <We will protect you, if necessary.>

Visser One was standing outside Dunkin' Donuts at 1:55 P.M.

At precisely 2:10 P.M., Chapman rounded the corner, dressed in a lime-green and yellow jogging outfit.

The Yeerk in my mother's head opened her hand. Her purse dropped. Chapman, always playing the role of pillar of the community, bent to pick it up for her. He straightened and held out the purse.

Visser One formed a smile. Then, the smile froze.

It was convincingly done.

Chapman said nothing. But I could see the blood draining out of his cheeks. He took a step back and then ran off double speed.

From my next perch, on the corrugated tin roof of Fred's Car Wash, I saw Chapman stop at a pay phone a block away and frantically punch the numbers.

Visser One stood fuming. She looked around again, trying to spot us. But there were pigeons and dogs and we could have been anywhere.

<Walk north one street,> Tobias said. <Embark on the large vehicle that stops at the next corner. Disembark at JCPenney.>

"It's called a 'bus,' you Andalite fool," she muttered in response. I happened to hear as she passed by below me.

Tobias's act was working.

<Good job, Tobias. You do a good Andalite. When the bus comes, you fly. I'll ride.>

<You're the boss,> Tobias said.

Two minutes later a bus pulled up against the painted yellow curb.

<Embark,> Tobias snapped.

<Embark?> I asked Tobias.

<I thought it sounded like something Ax would think was right.>

My mother got on the bus. I swooped down off the car wash and landed, scrabbling, on the hot metal roof of the bus. There was nothing to hold on to. But a couple of tiny rivets had popped out and I seized a precarious hold by prying my talon tips into the holes.

Not my favorite way to travel.

The bus rumbled back into traffic and began the five-minute ride to the mall. Fortunately it never got over ten or fifteen miles an hour. Ducking my head down and streamlining my body, I could resist the wind.

I could have kept pace from the air, which would have been a lot more comfortable.

Two blocks away from the stop in front of JCPenney, I lifted off. I flapped for altitude. An osprey near the ground sticks out.

I scanned the area for familiar faces. I spotted the hard stare of a peregrine falcon's eyes.

94

Jake was perched atop a bank out on the periphery of the mall parking lot.

<We're on schedule at this end,> I reported.

<You're sure Chapman saw her?>

<Oh, yeah, he saw her. He nearly wet himself.>

<Good. Were you followed?>

<We can only hope.>

<Any sign of her own forces?>

<We haven't exactly had time to watch everyone,> I said. <How about the others?>

<Rachel and Cassie are in place. Ax should be getting to the mountain soon. I think we can be confident that Erek will be there, on schedule.>

<Okay, Tobias?> I called.

<Yeah, I'm above you.>

<You can go, dude. We got it, here.>

<I've got it, here,> Jake corrected. <Don't forget, Marco. You stay quiet.>

<I know, I know,> I said, a little exasperated. <Don't let her hear my voice. Not even the one in my head.>

<That's right. The clothes are in that Dumpster.>

<You had to stash them in a Dumpster?>

<Hey, you wanted clothes, right?>

I flew to the Dumpster. It wasn't bad. I think

it was all boxes and stuff from the Gap and Old Navy. Much better than a restaurant Dumpster.

I demorphed in the Dumpster and pulled on the clothes Jake had stashed there.

Jake landed beside me.

<Fly, right?>

<That's the plan.>

Jake quickly demorphed, then morphed to fly. He buzzed his wings, took a few quick turns, then landed on my shoulder.

I climbed out and we hurried around to a side entrance of the JCPenney.

Visser One had walked from the bus stop through the door. She waited impatiently for instructions. She pretended to shop, tugging fitfully at some kids'-size Michael Jordan jerseys.

My size, maybe. Was she thinking about the son her host body had once had?

No, not likely. She was thinking about the fact that Controllers were everywhere. Thinking about the fact that by now Visser Three had a tail on her. Was watching her. Tightening his ring around her.

I lurked behind a tall potted plant. "Okay, directly ahead," I whispered to Jake. "There's a TV screen hanging down from above. Do you see it?"

Flies are very weak at seeing distances. It's why I had to be human. So I could act as an air traffic controller and direct Jake toward his target.

<I see bright, swirling lights, above and straight ahead.>

"That's the TV. Okay, she's in an almost straight line from here to the TV, just a shade to the right."

Jake took off. I lost sight of him immediately, of course. Hard to see a fly against the confused backdrop of visuals.

<I'm on her,> Jake announced a few moments later. <Beginning contact.>

Seconds later I heard Jake's thought-speak voice, sounding very different. And I saw my mother's head snap up.

<Go to the back of this establishment, Yeerk,> Jake instructed. <Purchase a neck protection garment. Also artificial skin designed for the protection of hands.>

Scarf and gloves. I almost laughed. It was classic Ax-ese.

Visser One must have said something harsh. The next thing I heard was Jake saying, <Do not be foolish, Yeerk. We are using this process to equip you as necessary. And to discover any pursuit. For your information we have spotted four human-Controllers who are already watching you.>

A lie, of course. But Visser One's head snapped around before she got control of herself.

<We are creating a trail, Yeerk,> Jake said with utter smugness. <And you are being watched, so do not attempt anything stupid. One wrong move and we'll kill you now and worry about Visser Three later.>

<Very nice,> I complimented Jake.

<Next stop, the camping store,> Jake said. <Let's see how well she holds up. She's volatile. She could go off.>

<No. She'll stick with the plan,> I said.

I understood Visser One. She saw the bright, clear line, too. Problem was, only one of us could be right.

CHAPTER 18

Rachel, her hair in two dorky braids and a goofy fisherman's cap low on her head, was staked out in Shoes and Handbags.

I was a few aisles over, in Hosiery. I looked slightly out of place. I could only hope that no one from school would spot me as I perused the racks of sheer-to-waist, sandal-foot taupe pantyhose.

That's the kind of thing that stays with you in school.

Visser One stormed into the Scarves, Gloves, and Hats department. She grabbed a gray wool scarf off a shelf, snatched a pair of woefully inadequate fancy leather gloves, and dutifully purchased them with a no-doubt-fake credit card.

99

Then she started to walk back toward the exit leading into the mall. All according to plan.

Then . . .

"Excuse me, ma'am? Could you follow me please?"

A security guard. Plainclothes. The kind of guy who always seems to end up following me through a store.

Rachel shot a glance at me. She raised a questioning eyebrow.

I moved closer, carefully, keeping out of Visser One's line of sight.

"Follow you?" my mother's voice snapped. "Why?"

"Just follow me, ma'am. I need to ask you some questions."

The Visser's hand drifted down toward her purse. The guard saw the movement, too.

"You are under arrest for stealing that scarf."

"I bought this scarf," the Visser said tightly. "I have the receipt."

The guard laughed nervously. He glanced around, like he was looking for help. But he sounded determined enough. "If you reach into your purse for the Dracon beam I'm sure you have, I will kill you right here and now, traitor."

Visser One's hand was in the purse.

The guard reached inside his coat.

We were about two seconds away from a shoot-out in a crowded store.

Suddenly Rachel was behind me. "Hide, you idiot. You're gaping like a tourist! I have this," Rachel whispered.

She was right. I was standing in the open, drawn toward her without realizing it. If my mother had turned . . .

I ducked behind a display of long velvet shawls.

Rachel moved fast. She locked her hand around Visser One's wrist. Then, in a loud, nasal whine, she said, "I saw you buy that scarf!"

The guard hesitated. Visser One stiffened. She stared closely at Rachel, but Rachel had turned away.

"This woman is being arrested, and she didn't do anything! Lady! Lady! You sold her that scarf, now she's being arrested! What kind of a store is this?"

One thing we couldn't do: leave any Controller behind who could recognize us and wonder. Rachel was avoiding eye contact, hiding beneath her hat and bad hair. Hiding behind a false voice.

I hoped it was enough.

"It's ridiculous! This woman is being arrested and she paid for it! She paid too much, if you ask me, for that fabric. It's not cashmere, after all!"

I smothered a grin.

It was working. A crowd was gathering. The saleswoman was in it now, agreeing that Visser One had paid for the scarf.

<What is going on?> Jake wondered, confused.

It's hard to follow conversations when you're a fly. But of course we couldn't answer him.

Rachel moved out of the crowd and grabbed my arm.

"Let's get out of here."

"No one is watching —"

"Security cameras," she hissed. She nodded toward the ceiling. I saw the dark glass blister that hid a camera.

"Oh."

I followed Rachel toward a dressing room.

My first and probably last visit to a women's dressing room.

Rachel led me out a back door. Into a maintenance walkway, all cinder block and steel doors.

We reached the camping store before Visser One and Jake did. Cassie was waiting there.

She ran interference as Visser One was put through her paces buying climbing rope and pitons.

Rachel and I drifted around, pretending to shop. We were watching the others in the store. Watching those who were watching Visser One.

Jake had bluffed earlier, claiming that we'd spotted four human-Controllers on Visser One's tail.

That was no longer a lie. Within minutes we were confident that the true number was not four, but five.

"You wanted to make sure she was followed, Marco. She's being followed. And now we are setting up one heck of a shoot-out at the OK Corral," Rachel whispered. "You'd sure better know what you're doing."

"Yeah. I'd better."

CHAPTER 19

She had ropes and pitons, gloves and boots.

She had a tail of human-Controllers behind her as she drove the rented Audi from the mall out of town, toward the distant mountains.

The OK Corral.

All of us were in the car with the exception of Tobias and Ax.

We were in roach morph, crawling beneath the driver's seat.

Fuzzy black carpet was like tall grass beneath my six legs. A long-forgotten, open roll of peppermint Lifesavers was a huge log, its diameter far longer than we were tall.

Way, way overhead, as high as clouds, was the steel tube and coiled spring underside of the seat. Too far away to see more than huge, indistinct shadows were gigantic feet and ankles pressing on high-rise pedals.

She knew we were with her. She didn't know where we were, but she knew we were watching her.

"Why don't we merely take a helicopter to this Hork-Bajir colony?" she asked.

<You assume the colony is located somewhere high up?> Cassie took over the job of communication. We needed to put Visser One off her guard. Needed her to begin to see us as allies. Cassie was the one for that job.

"Obviously," Visser One snapped. "Am I a fool? Ropes? Pitons?"

<You would not find it from the air. It is in a narrow, hidden valley high in the mountains. Trees would block a simple human helicopter.> She paused. <Your troops, when they arrive, will need to cut their way in.>

"My troops?"

<We are not fools, either,> Cassie said. <You do not intend to merely arrest or discredit Visser Three. You intend to kill him. We both know that with his morphing ability he is far more powerful than you, with your unstable human host body.>

"I can deal with Visser Three."

<Can you? We have tried many times. And yet, he still lives.>

"Humility? From an Andalite?"

<Realism from an Andalite,> Cassie said.

Visser One barked out a laugh. "You're afraid of him."

<Tell her, "yes,"> I said privately to Cassie. <Tell her he's killed a lot of us.>

<Yes. We were far more numerous, once. Many of us have died fighting Visser Three.>

A lie, of course. But it sounded real enough. Visser One would latch on to the information. She would think we were fools for revealing it.

We wanted her to think us fools.

"Do you imagine I will be more gentle when I am in power, again?"

I started to tell Cassie what to say. But she was already there, ahead of me.

<No. We simply think you will be weaker,> Cassie said. <The disruption of command will work to our benefit. And in direct battle you will be easier to kill than Visser Three. Humans, Controllers or not, die easily.>

Again, it had the feel of honesty. The insult would make it seem honest.

And it had the added benefit of focusing my mother . . . Visser One . . . on the danger of Visser Three. We were reminding her just how deadly Visser Three could be.

"And yet . . ." Visser One mused. "And yet, the

casualty reports from Earth are always weighted heavily toward Hork-Bajir and Taxxons. In fact . . . I am trying to recall when I have ever seen a report listing a human-Controller casualty."

My guts were ice.

We had made a mistake. We had made a terrible mistake.

<What do I say?> Cassie demanded.

<I . . . I . . .> My brain wouldn't work. The thoughts wouldn't form into any sort of order.

Visser One had just put her finger on our greatest secret.

<Say *something*!> Rachel yelled.

<No, too late,> Jake interrupted. <Too late. Let it go. No choice.>

"Well, well, well," Visser One said.

She knew.

There was only one reason why a group of Andalite guerrilla fighters would inflict more casualties on Hork-Bajir than on humans: The Andalite guerillas weren't Andalites.

A human would spare a human life.

<She knows,> Jake said. <Or at least suspects.>

<Yeah.>

<Marco . . .>

<Nothing changes,> I said harshly. <She was going down before. She's still going down.>

Not true. Before it had all been abstract. It had all been about the solution, the line from A to B.

Now it was about survival. No one could know the truth about us. It would bring our annihilation.

No one could know what we were, and live.

CHAPTER 20

Visser One drove like a madwoman. The Audi tore around hairpin mountain curves at speeds that would have been high on a freeway.

The roll of peppermint Lifesavers had become a menace. With every wild turn or braking it rolled suddenly, a redwood log coming downhill at us.

<Has your mother always driven like this?> Rachel asked.

<My mother is not driving,> I said coldly. But she was. My mom *had* always been a wild driver. It used to make my dad crazy. This was the Yeerk tapping into the human host's brain.

<Maybe so,> I amended. No need to start a

fight with Rachel. <Maybe that *is* the way she used to drive.>

<Yeah? Now I know where you get your driving skills.>

Rachel, being nice. I laughed to myself. When Rachel started being nice it meant things were really bad.

Visser One took a hard right and the ride turned bumpy.

An understatement.

The carpet jumped beneath us. We used our roach legs as shock absorbers, but there was a lot of shock to absorb. Wild vibrations that translated to the roach mind as danger.

Suddenly, mercifully, the car stopped.

"I have followed your directions. Andalites," she said.

The final word was said with a half laugh.

<We must be at the Visitors' Center,> I said.

<Good,> Rachel said. <I'm carsick.>

<Unpack the items you purchased. Begin to walk along the main trail.>

"Visser Three's forces will be all over me in seconds!" she protested.

<No. They'll track you,> Jake said. <They won't move till he himself is here.>

"Tell that to the fool back at the mall!"

<He acted out of panic. He wasn't expecting you.>

Visser One got out of the car and slammed the door. We waited until enough time had passed for the Visser to grab her gear from the trunk, change into the hiking boots, scarf, and gloves and start up the trail.

<Let's go,> Jake said. <Rachel? You're first. Keep low.>

Rachel motored out from under the seat onto the back floor mat. She began demorphing immediately, growing, sliding, shifting to keep her mutating limbs from being caught in the tight space back there.

Mostly I saw her feet. They filled my vision. Bare, of course. We'd never learned to morph shoes.

Her head eventually rose above the seat back. "Okay," she said. "We're clear. For now."

<Okay. Morph and go.>

Rachel tried to roll down the window. But of course it was power, and Visser One had taken the keys. She cracked the door on the passenger side. She morphed to bald eagle and took off, racing to her appointed position.

If Tobias had not made it, Rachel would. If both made it, so much the better.

Cassie, Jake, and I spread out throughout the car and began to demorph. If we'd all stayed in one place and demorphed we'd have ended up as sardines.

I demorphed on the passenger side. My head rose from the gruesome mass of bug exoskeleton. I could see through the windshield. Really see. Like a human.

She'd chosen a parking space distant from the few other parked cars. Good and bad for us. No one would spot us on the way to their own car. But we'd have a long, open walk to the trailhead.

I looked around. Rachel was just clearing the nearest trees.

I spotted Visser One moving speedily toward the trail. She'd always kept in good shape, my mom. Although sailing had been her thing, not hiking.

Jake was in the driver's seat. "Okay. We go straight to bird morphs. The bad guys won't be far behind us."

"Or far ahead, either," I said, nodding toward the dwindling figure of Visser One.

"One at a time or we'll look like a bird-of-prey convention," Cassie said.

I began to morph to osprey. I was closest to the open door. A few minutes later I was all feathers and talons. I fluttered out through the door, landed on the gravel, and flapped into the air.

I wasn't ten feet up before I saw it: a long, black limousine. It was entering the parking lot.

No one goes camping or hiking in a limo.

<Visser Three!> I said. <Heads down. He's here!>

I continued flapping, flapping, fighting dead air, feeling conspicuous.

Not that there weren't birds of prey in the forest. But Visser Three knew by now to look out for hawks and eagles.

The limo skidded to a stop, spraying gravel. Behind it, three big SUV's.

The limo window rolled down. I was maybe thirty feet up, forty feet downwind from the Audi.

A hand thrust out of the limo window. Osprey eyes saw it clearly. Saw what it was holding.

<Jake! Cassie!> I yelled.

TSEEEEEW!

The Dracon beam fired. The front of the Audi sizzled, fried, and disintegrated.

<NOOOO!> I cried.

TSEEEEEW!

Ka-BOOOM!

A fireball exploded from the Audi's gas tank. The entire car, what was left of it, erupted upward, spun halfway on its axis, and landed on the gravel.

It was a charred shell before it hit the ground.

CHAPTER 21

<Jake! Cassie!>

No answer. Nothing. Silence. Silence but for the crackling of the fire.

<Rachel!> I yelled. <Jake and Cassie are . . . I think . . .>

But Rachel was already out of thought-speak range.

Slam! Slam! Slam!

Doors opened and closed and the human-Controllers piled out of the SUV's. Boots hit gravel.

Chapman climbed out of the limo and joined the guys coming from the SUV's.

And then, last, came a human who was no human.

Visser Three in human morph.

He looked around, barely sparing a glance at the burning wreck of a car. A park ranger was running from the Visitors' Center.

The Visser jerked his head.

TSEEEEW!

The ranger sizzled and disappeared.

Then, I felt those cold eyes on me. At this distance his voice was faint. If I'd been human I'd never have heard my death sentence.

"The bird," he said. "Kill the bird."

TSEEEEW! TSEEEEW!

To my left! To my right!

The Dracon beams scorched the air on either side of me.

Two seconds for them to aim again. One, one thousand . . . Two, one thousand . . .

I jerked left.

TSEEEEEW! TSEEEEEW!

Misses, far to one side. And now I was farther away. The nearest tree was only fifteen feet away.

TSEEEEEW! TSEEEEEW!

Just in front of my face branches burst into flame.

I flared, lost speed, and dropped. I used the momentum of my fall to whip hard around the tree trunk and zoom wildly, inches off the pine needles.

The Yeerks wouldn't get another shot at me. Not now.

Oh, God. Jake! Cassie!

The burning car was burning right inside my brain. The aluminum skin had been evaporated, leaving nothing but the bones of the car. Bare aluminum posts and fire.

And, though I had not seen them except in my imagination, the singed, heat-cracked bones of my friends.

What now? I asked myself. What now?

The plan. Was there still a plan?

I tried to think. But I could no longer see the bright, clear line. All I could see was flame.

Visser Three. I'd been so busy worrying about Visser One I had forgotten that he was our main enemy. I'd intended to harass and trick and distract Visser One into carelessness. But I had tricked myself.

Visser Three was going to win. He was going to kill my mother. And he would not die. He would kill her, and he would not die. I would have set up my own mother for murder by my own worst enemy.

No. No. That couldn't be. I had to think. Had to think.

Tobias, maybe. Rachel, maybe. They were the next step.

Ax. Where was Ax? Clearing the place of campers? Scouting the location?

Where? What were they doing? How . . .

116

Show me the line, I begged. Show me the A to B.

My friends. My mother . . .

All my fault. And now I was lost. Nothing to do but stand and watch the horrible drama play out.

No. No, the awful voice in my head said. The line was still bright and clear. The plan still worked. If Ax and Erek had done their jobs the plan could still work.

Only one thing needed to be changed: I would have to play the part of Jake.

CHAPTER 22

I flew ahead to the appointed rendezvous. I passed over Visser One on the way. She was still moving quickly up the hill. Had she heard the explosion? Did she feel the fear eating at her, the fear that death was coming up behind her?

Or was she filled with anticipation? Was she giddy and energized with the thought of killing her foe, of annihilating the free Hork-Bajir, of living to dance on Visser Three's grave?

I pulled far ahead. I headed for the clearing halfway up the mountain. There was a cluster of lean-tos for campers on the edge of the clearing. Ax, using his morphing ability, should already have frightened them from the area.

We didn't want innocents caught in the cross

fire. We didn't want bystanders hurt. That was our plan.

<Tell that to that ranger back there, Marco,> I said to myself. <Tell it to his family. No innocent bystanders in our little war. No place for them, is there? No time to think about the damage you do with our bright, clear line.>

A campfire smoldered below. In one of the shelters two sleeping bags were spread over bunk beds. Two backpacks sat propped against the wall. These nature lovers had left in a hurry.

Ax at work. Maybe. Or maybe Visser Three's forces had come in from this direction as well. More innocents. Dead, or merely terrified?

We'd chosen Wildwood Trail specifically because it wasn't popular. It wasn't very scenic. It wouldn't be wall-to-wall crunchies working out their Timberlands.

And because, a mile or so up, we could cut away from the trail and go cross-country through terrain that would thin out the pursuit.

I spotted Visser One laboring up the slope, fighting the gravity I could easily defy. Her pretty face was dripping sweat. Her lungs gasped.

That was the plan, too. Too rushed, too scared, too tired to think. And yet, she already knew too much. She'd figured out what Visser Three had not.

It was weird, perverse, maybe. But I was

proud of her. As if it had been my mother, and not the Yeerk in her head, who had penetrated our deepest secret.

I caught an updraft and soared high into the air. Up into the clean, clear air.

I wanted to keep flying. Just catch a breeze and sail away and leave it all behind. But how could I? How could I, with the possibility of Jake and Cassie being dead?

<No, no, Marco,> I sneered. <Far better that they should die to bring about more death. Yes, that would give their lives meaning.>

I rose high and searched the trail ahead. But not even osprey eyes could penetrate the dense foliage. I did not spot Ax or Tobias or Rachel.

Below, far back down at the trailhead, Visser Three was still in his human morph. He was moving swiftly up the trail. A dozen armed men before him, a dozen more behind him.

But one man was out in front, all alone, moving very fast. He wore a camouflage jacket and blue jeans. A camouflage stocking cap was pulled down, hiding most of his red hair.

The way he was moving he was either an athlete or a very experienced woodsman. He left the trail and went cross-country.

Either going ahead to take a shot at Visser One. Or going ahead to spy out what was happening.

I'd have to watch Red-hair. He made me nervous.

I knew that what I saw was not even the thin edge of Visser Three's true forces. I knew that the sky above me was dotted with shielded Bug fighters. And maybe the Blade ship as well. Not to mention any of Visser One's loyal troops.

The killing had only taken a rest break. It would start again once Visser Three was sure of Visser One's goal. Once all her forces were in the open and committed. Once he was sure of victory.

I circled back to the campsite. Visser One had been instructed to wait there. I floated down, skimmed in, hidden from the Visser's sight. I landed in the middle branches of a tall pine.

Only then did I see the goblin form of a Hork-Bajir, standing perfectly still. So still it could have been a statue.

<Rachel? Tobias?> I called.

<Rachel,> she answered. <Haven't seen Tobias, yet.>

<I'm here,> a thought-speak voice answered. <Right above you, Marco.>

I jerked my head upward. The seven-foot-tall, bladed form rested comfortably another twenty feet up the trunk.

<You guys forget: Hork-Bajir are arboreal. Why be on the ground when you can have some altitude?>

<Where are Jake and Cassie?> Rachel asked.
I didn't answer. I couldn't.
<Marco?> Rachel pressed.
I couldn't. Couldn't say it.
<Marco!>
<Visser Three. He got them.>
<What?> Tobias cried. <Captured?>
<No. No. I don't think so.>

CHAPTER 23

We waited. Silent. Dangerous.

I know Rachel. I know she wanted action, not playacting. I knew she would explode at the smallest provocation.

I know Tobias. I knew that in the face of so much sadness he would retreat from his human side. I knew that he was more hawk now than ever, despite his Hork-Bajir morph.

And what could I say to them? What could I say to lead them? Or control them?

Nothing. Because I know myself, too. I knew that I was scared and desperate and that my insides were being eaten away. I knew that I was focusing all my mind, all my thoughts on the plan, the plan, the plan, shutting out all other thoughts.

I had nothing to say to Rachel or Tobias. They would do, or not do, whatever they chose.

Visser One wandered warily through the abandoned campsite. I saw her as Rachel saw her: the enemy. One of the Yeerk invaders who had cost her the life of her cousin and her best friend.

She was a dozen feet away, two long strides away, from Rachel's Hork-Bajir blades.

Rachel stepped into the open.

Tobias dropped easily from the tree, landing on T-rex feet.

My mother . . . Visser One . . . swung her backpack forward and reached inside. The Dracon weapon was in her hand in a flash.

I breathed.

Rachel was letting her live. For now. Fast as Visser One had been, she'd never have reached her weapon had Rachel not wanted her to.

"You . . ." Rachel said, stepping forward and speaking in the Hork-Bajir voice. "Where are Andalite friends?"

"Your friends are fine, Maska Fettan," the Visser responded.

"My name. You know my name," Rachel said, sounding relieved. Then, a slow Hork-Bajir scowl. "Andalite friends say password. All must speak password."

I spotted a movement so slight only a hawk would have seen it. Red-hair. Only the red hair was hidden now by the camouflage ski mask he'd pulled down over his face.

He was in a stand of bushes. Close enough to see. Not to hear. He had a Dracon beam in his hand. But the way he held it was for self-defense, not attack.

"Freedom now, freedom forever," Visser One recited with an amused sneer.

"Yes." Rachel smiled, if you can call what Hork-Bajir do when they're happy smiling. "You are friend."

"Yes. I am a friend to all free Hork-Bajir." The Visser could hardly resist masking my mother's face with a grin of glee. "How is the free colony faring, Maska Fettan?"

"Good, good! All free now. All happy. Much bark to eat," Rachel said.

"That's good. Love to hear that the bark is tasty," Visser One said, dripping contempt. "Now, conduct me to the colony, as you were instructed to do."

"You change to bird. Fly. Human slow walker."

"Sadly, I am ill," Visser One said. She made a little cough. "I am unable to morph at the moment. I will have to travel as a human."

"Human slow," Tobias interjected with true Hork-Bajir dimness.

"Yes, yes, it's all a mess," Visser One agreed testily. "I wish I could morph to bird and fly, but since that is not possible, perhaps you two geniuses could follow the orders you were given."

"Andalite friend says, 'Take her to colony,'" Tobias said.

"Yes," Rachel agreed.

"Up there." Tobias pointed off the trail. He pointed up toward a high, naked rock summit. "Up there is place. Up there Andalite friends hide colony."

A naked rock peak. The perfect place to stage a battle that would involve forces on the ground and in the air. The perfect place for an Animorph.

"Up there?" Visser One said slowly. Her eyes narrowed. "Holograms. Cloaking shields? Yes, of course. Few human interlopers, and camouflage and a force field would stop them. It would work. A small, deep valley most likely. Invisible from the ground because of the altitude. Easily concealed from the air or space by Andalite countermeasures. The energy drain would be immense, but not unmanageable. . . ."

I would have smiled. Yes, Visser One, just what I hoped you'd think.

Welcome to the OK Corral, Visser One.

CHAPTER 24

I'd seen enough. Visser One had fallen for it. So far.

Rachel and Tobias would handle the rest of the climb. It was unlikely the Visser would try to harm the two Hork-Bajir before she had been shown the way to the colony. Unlikely, but not impossible. She was armed. And I knew what Visser One was. Ruthless. Cruel. That she wore the face of my mother — the woman who had taught me about laughter — was a grotesque irony.

<See, *that's* ironic, Alanis,> I muttered to no one.

The ascent would take hours. Tobias and Rachel would have to slip away whenever possible to demorph and remorph. If Ax was nearby, on-station, it would work. He would substitute. One Hork-Bajir looked much like the next, but this substitution would be even more perfect than that. Some weeks ago, on a friendly visit with the free Hork-Bajir, Ax had acquired the same Hork-Bajir DNA Rachel was using. Not even a Hork-Bajir would notice any difference.

I drifted back down the hill. Back down toward Visser Three and his Controllers.

His force was growing. I don't know how they'd gotten there, but a force of Hork-Bajir was moving up the hill from the right flank, swinging through trees and marching along the ground. I counted thirty before I gave up.

This would complicate things. I'd hoped to isolate the two Vissers. Visser One, prepared as we had prepared her with ropes and pitons, would be able to climb. So would Visser Three who would simply morph something capable.

The jagged, naked rocks would delay the human-Controllers. But Hork-Bajir were strong. And, according to the Hork-Bajir we knew, they came from a planet where life existed entirely within impossibly steep canyons.

The Hork-Bajir-Controllers would be able to keep pace with Rachel and Tobias. Only a limited number of Bug fighters could be brought to bear within the limited space, so the balance of power on the ground was important.

Too much on Visser Three's side of the equation and he'd win without suffering much himself. And now, the wild card, we Animorphs, were reduced. Thirty Hork-Bajir-Controllers and a dozen human-Controllers, plus Visser Three. It was more than we could handle.

Far back down the trail, Red-hair rejoined Visser Three. So now Visser Three knew that Visser One had linked up with two Hork-Bajir.

Would he put it all together? Would Visser Three realize that these were free Hork-Bajir? That Visser One was on her way to the free colony?

It was getting to be time for me to change morphs. The air was thin, the updrafts nonexistent at this altitude. Flying was a chore. And soon I would stand out all too obviously.

<Where is Ax?> I wondered. <Rachel? Tobias? Have you seen Ax?>

<No,> Rachel said.

<He was supposed to do his best to clear the area then rejoin us,> I said in frustration.

<Plan not working out so well, General?>

<Just get Visser One up that mountain.>

<Face it, Marco, it's a fiasco. It's a total fiasco! We're dragging this woman up the moun-

tain for what? It'd be so easy to just give her a shove off the trail.>

<Shut up, Rachel!> I yelled. <Just shut up!>

<Oh yeah, you're calm and in control,> Rachel taunted. <Jake's gone. Cassie's gone. And the person running this mission is working on setting up his own *mother*? This is a waste of time. Marco, just fly off somewhere. Just get out of range so you don't have to see what I'm —>

<Rachel, that's enough,> Tobias said quietly.

I couldn't believe what I was "hearing." Tobias never messes with Rachel. I think Rachel was shocked, too.

<Marco has enough load on his shoulders,> Tobias said. <I trust him.>

<You trust him? You trust *him*?!>

<You just want Visser One?> Tobias said. <Or do you want them both? We need this woman alive as bait.>

All the while I could see Visser One scrambling over rocks, climbing, hauling herself up by roots and low branches. And Tobias and Rachel were with her, one ahead, one behind.

<Yeah, his plan's worked out so well so far,> Rachel said. But she fell silent after that.

I put her out of my mind. Besides, she was right. The plan was falling apart. I needed reinforcements.

Where was Ax? Where was the Andalite?

CHAPTER 25

I'd been a long time in morph. A quick check on Visser Three, and I would abandon the osprey.

Visser Three himself was still with his group of human-Controllers. They were slowing down, worn out by sliding in their street shoes.

But the Visser was no longer concerned with shoes. He had reverted to his Andalite host body. He was a nimble, dangerous deer.

No one was sweating more than Chapman. I almost felt sorry for him. But not too sorry. If all went well, my school would be needing a new assistant principal next week.

I circled behind them, staying out of sight as well as I could. I drifted close enough to hear scattered bits of conversation.

Some of it was very interesting.

"Let's kill her now," Chapman urged, gasping like a fish out of water. "Before they get away."

<Why, because you are weak and tired? No,> Visser Three said. <She is heading for the Hork-Bajir fugitives. I know it! Either to unite with them, or to prove their existence to the Council of Thirteen and discredit me. I will have her *and* the Hork-Bajir fugitives!>

"But, Visser, in these human host bodies, lacking equipment, we may be unable to keep up with you," Chapman said very respectfully.

<Am I blind? Am I a fool? Two columns of Hork-Bajir and Taxxons are even now converging. If you fall by the wayside, so be it. I will not be denied my victory!>

Evidently encouraged by Visser Three's seemingly tolerant mood, another human-Controller made the mistake of offering an opinion.

"It's hard to believe that these Hork-Bajir hosts could form a colony right under our noses. How did we —"

The Andalite tail blade whipped and stopped, quivering, pressed against the man's right leg.

"No, I —" the man cried. "I meant no criticism! No!"

"Visser, we need every man who can fire a weapon," Chapman intervened.

<Yes, you are right, Chapman,> Visser Three said. <It would be foolish to cut off his leg. How would he walk without a leg?>

The man almost had time to breathe a sigh of relief. Then Visser Three whipped his tail again. The man's left arm fell to the ground.

<You all will only hinder my progress,> Visser Three spat. <I will proceed alone from here. The Hork-Bajir and Taxxons will join us soon. And the fleet stands ready. Catch up when your frail bodies allow. I have a morph that will do very nicely for this challenge.>

With his entourage watching, Visser Three began to morph.

Squeeeeesh!

His Andalite head flattened to the shape of a B-movie flying saucer. His main eyes closed and sealed. His stalk eyes remained but thickened. The eyeballs bulged and reddened.

Multijointed legs sprouted from his sides. One, two, three — six, total, replacing his quick-disappearing Andalite legs and hooves.

His blue-and-tan Andalite fur seemed to be absorbed into him, as though it had been sucked in.

What remained was a translucent skin or shell of no particular color.

The legs lengthened, becoming spindly, almost like a spider's. The two front legs ended in claws. The back four legs ended in sharp, barbed spikes.

And then, before my startled gaze, the shell began to change. From a translucence that revealed vague, distorted blue, red, and orange shadows of his internal organs, it became green and brown.

It became the precise green of the trees overhead. The exact brown of the trail.

<A chameleon!> I whispered.

The Visser's bizarre, spindly land crab was nearly invisible, even to my eyes. The colors and patterns of its shell shifted as rapidly as it walked.

Okay, Marco, you knew he'd morph something dangerous. That still fits the plan.

Of course, I hadn't known he'd be nearly invisible.

CHAPTER 26

I landed and demorphed well off the trail.

Strange to be here, so high up. It was quiet. A few birds sang. The breeze rustled the sparse tall grass. The trees sighed.

"All I need is a picnic," I said, wanting to hear the sound of my own voice. "Some chips. A ham sandwich."

Jake and Cassie, burned in Visser One's SUV.

Ax missing.

My mother . . .

I could run away. Leave town. Never come back. I had the powers. I could get by. I could go to Hollywood. Or France. Somewhere.

French Marco. I liked it. Were the Yeerks in

France? I didn't care. I wouldn't pay any attention to them.

"Oh, God," I moaned. I put my face in my hands.

<Marco! You are very badly located!>

My head snapped up. I looked around, confused, till I saw the northern harrier floating on the slight breeze.

"Ax?" I said, not that he could hear me.

<Marco, a column of Hork-Bajir and Taxxons is coming up the opposite side of this ridge. In approximately two of your minutes they will be able to see you.>

"They're not *my* minutes, you alien nitwit, they're everyone's minutes!"

But I was busy morphing. Not to osprey again. Wings were of diminishing usefulness now. But I still needed to be able to stay out in front of humans, Hork-Bajir, and whatever strange thing Visser Three had become.

Time for the goat.

Ax had floated lower. He kept to the air, but he could hear me now.

<I discern that the arrival of these additional forces so early in the plan may have created an imbalance that will affect our plans in a negative way,> Ax said.

"Gee, do you think?!" I yelled.

<We need reinforcements.>

"You know some private army you can call, 'cause if you do, now would be the time!" I yelled.

It was sarcastic. I didn't expect him to take me seriously. But before I could object, Ax had caught the breeze and was heading downhill, letting gravity give him speed.

"What the . . . What are you doing?" I screamed.

Insane! I'd found Ax and lost him within a minute!

"Okay, okay, get a grip," I told myself shakily. "Get a grip. Okay. Figure it out. Back to Rachel and Tobias and Visser One. The only thing to do. Morph. Come on, Marco, focus!"

I focused on the memory of the big mountain goat, asleep in its safe little zoo habitat.

Stupid, but I was ticked at that goat.

Morphing is never logical, never neat and clean and orderly. The changes don't necessarily start at the head and move on to the toes, though they can. And this time, they did.

Sprooot!

Two sharp, daggerlike black horns sprouted from the top of my head.

I felt an itchiness on my face. I raised my hand and felt a long, rather soft white beard beneath my chin.

The five toes on each of my feet melded together to form two big padded toes, toes that could spread to help the mountain goat keep its balance on snowy, rocky slopes.

White fur began to grow up my legs, which were becoming the stocky, sturdy back legs of the goat. Over the soft, fluffy fur grew coarser hair, protection against wind and rain.

Suddenly, I tipped forward. I fell on my hands, now also split hooves with rough pads underneath.

Screeeesh!

My small human shoulders heaved upward into the powerful, shaggy shoulders of the almost three-hundred-pound male mountain goat.

I felt the mountain goat's mind merge within my own. But I wasn't interested in fighting it. The goat wanted to climb, and so did I.

I bounded off across the sparse, rocky soil. Up, up, straight up.

The power in my legs was incredible! I wasn't climbing against the pull of gravity. Gravity was irrelevant! It didn't exist!

Up through the trees. Leaping easily, playfully over boulders that would have taken a human five minutes to clamber cautiously over.

My legs were pile drivers. I was on pogo sticks, just bouncing, bounding, springing, practically flying.

I spotted and smelled the Hork-Bajir as they

crested the ridge, but who cared? They'd never get me. This mountain was mine. These rocks belonged to me!

Up and up, pulling effortlessly away from the Hork-Bajir, I drew level with Visser One and my two friends. They had deployed ropes and pitons now. Visser One was being pushed and hauled like a sack of potatoes.

They climbed the easier path. I took a much harder way. A way with no trail, with scrappy miniature trees blocking my way, with no visible footholds, with tumbling gravel and crumbling rocks.

I went the way that no human climber, no expert rock climber armed with every piece of equipment could have climbed in under half a day.

It was an escalator to me.

My eyes spotted every minuscule crevice. My hooves caught every crack. I hauled three hundred pounds of goat up a sheer wall so easily that I might have been Tinkerbell floating upward on magic dust.

I passed Visser One.

Rachel spotted me.

<Marco?>

<Who else?>

<Yeah. Good luck, okay?>

<No problem-o, Xena,> I said.

CHAPTER 27

I waited atop the mountain, alone. King of the world.

From the peak, the back side of the mountain extended almost flat toward the west. All I saw was a long slope that extended perhaps a quarter of a mile before seeming to be broken by the spine of a ridge.

We had come up the east face. A nearly sheer drop. The southeast and northeast were no better — sheer cliffs.

A fatal fall in three directions.

A fatal fall for a human. Or human-Controller.

Nothing that looked remotely like a hidden valley. Nothing that looked remotely like a secret Hork-Bajir colony.

140

But then, that was to be expected.

My mother's face appeared very suddenly above the rocks to the east. She was being pushed up from beneath. She clambered up, clearly exhausted.

For a while she just lay flat on her back, gasping and coughing. Rachel and Tobias rose up behind her.

Then she rolled over and with sheer willpower made her body stand.

Once again I felt that strange pride. Even with Rachel and Tobias to help, it was an amazing accomplishment climbing this peak.

A fitting end. The last exertion, the last effort.

So easy for me now. I could throw my three hundred pounds forward, lower my head, slam into her, send her flying, arms windmilling helplessly as she fell and fell and fell . . .

The Visser would die.

His helpless host, my mother, as well.

"Andalite?" she panted.

<Of course,> I said. Be so careful, Marco, I warned myself. This was to be Jake's role. He was to talk to her. She can't know who you are.

But what did it matter now? It was over. It would end here.

It would matter because knowing at last that we had tricked her, she might call my name. She might say "Marco."

"Marco! Don't let them kill me, Marco!"

I shuddered.

I was lost. Her life would end here. So would mine, I now knew. How could I live? How could I live, knowing?

"Well, Andalite or human, or whatever you are behind that morph, you'd better know one thing: My loyal forces fill the sky! Betray me and you'll be blasted apart!"

<We have a deal,> I said blandly. <Visser Three will soon join us. He will be alone, or nearly alone.>

"The Hork-Bajir colony. I don't see any colony!"

<Erek,> I said privately, <I hope you're here, dude.> Then, in open thought-speak, <Not to get all *Prince of Egypt* on you, but . . . Behold!>

The ground of the western slope shimmered. Then it disappeared. Visser One actually jumped back. The valley appeared just before her feet.

"Hork-Bajir home," Rachel said, still playing her part.

Below us, beneath impossibly steep cliff walls, a lush valley teemed with free Hork-Bajir.

I watched the sick, eager smile spread across my mother's beautiful face as Visser One peered into the valley below.

Several young Hork-Bajir swung through the trees, playing a game of tag. Adult Hork-Bajir stripped bark from the trunks of the tall pines. I counted at least forty or fifty Hork-Bajir going about their daily routine.

<Okay, we fulfilled our end of the bargain,> I muttered. <Now it's up to Visser Three.>

She smiled, right at me. "I know you. I know you, don't I?"

<I am an Andalite warrior. That's all you need to know.>

"No. Andalites don't make jokes. Let alone human popular culture references. No, you're a human. And . . ." She searched her memory, rolling her eyes up. "Someone I knew, once. Long ago, maybe. But someone I knew."

CHAPTER 28

$\mathbf{I}$ froze. Stiff. Still.

I wanted her to say my name.

I'd given myself away. Deliberately. I wanted her to say my name. I wanted her to call out to me, to say, "Marco, I love you, I miss you, I'm still your —"

Oh, God, I had messed up. The plan, I'd ruined it, just to hear her say my name. I'd been fooling myself. I couldn't do it.

<It's okay, Marco,> a gentle voice said. But not my mom. Rachel. <It's okay, man. It's okay.>

Then, everything happened at once.

Above the lip of the mountaintop he rose, grotesque, half sky-blue, half the color of bare rock.

Visser Three climbed up.

<Well, well, well,> he said. <What's this? Visser One perched on the edge of a free Hork-Bajir colony? Chatting amiably with two free Hork-Bajir and, unless I miss my guess, an Andalite?>

She spun to face him. No fear. "It's over, you incompetent fraud! My loyal ships are above us."

<So are mine,> Visser Three hissed. <And they will blow your ships from the sky!>

"So typical of you. You think only of brute violence. Fool. My ships are making a sensor record. They have recorded this valley, this colony of free Hork-Bajir! What do you think the Council of Thirteen will say when they see it?"

Visser Three showed no emotion. Most likely he couldn't.

Visser One reached into her backpack. Out came not a weapon but what looked a bit like a cell phone.

"This is Visser One," she said. "Attack!"

<Yes, by all means, attack me,> Visser Three said with a laugh. <My ships, too, are making a sensor record. A record of the traitor, the former Visser One firing on loyal Yeerks!>

Suddenly, the sky overhead seemed to part, like a cloth being torn at the seam, and there appeared a ship like none I had ever seen.

Huge! Larger than Visser Three's Blade ship.

It had eight pods arranged around a central, cylindrical core. Four massive engines bunched at the rear, blazing blue fire.

<A Nova-class Empire ship?> Visser Three gasped.

Just then, streaking out of the west, came a stream of smaller ships, Visser Three's Bug fighters. Visser One whirled to watch them, a swarm moving quickly across the back of the mountain range. Among them, a giant battle-ax: the Blade ship of Visser Three.

The squadrons flew low over the colony.

"Visser Three!" my mother yelled. "You are under arrest for criminal incompetence!"

<Traitor!> Visser Three roared.

He lunged, front claws snapping.

Visser One drew a Dracon beam.

Visser Three's Bug fighters sped toward Visser One's descending armada. The battle erupted. The sky was ripped by massive Dracon cannon firing, as Bug fighters and the Blade ship circled around Visser One's Empire ship.

Visser One fired.

Visser Three sliced.

<Aaaarrgghh!>

A sizzling hole appeared in Visser Three's color-shifting shell.

My mother screamed. She staggered and fell. Her clothes were stained red.

<NOOOO!> I cried. I leaped. Leaped at Visser Three, head down, horns ready.

<Marco! Stop!> Rachel cried. <It's the plan! It has to happen! It has to happen! She has to —>

<NOOOOOO!> I slammed into the chameleon morph. It jerked back. Visser Three staggered. Three legs crumpled.

Visser One fired.

The shot missed Visser Three. It hit me.

Searing pain. There was a neat semicircle of flesh gone from my haunch. I staggered, blinded and disoriented by the pain.

"Destroy the colony! The colony!" my mother screamed into her communicator. "Don't fire on Visser Three's ships! The colony! Kill them all! Kill them all!"

<Pathetic attempt. You can't hope to conceal your treason,> Visser Three said.

TSEEEEEEW! TSEEEEEEW!

Dracon cannon were firing from the sky above. The Empire ship was blasting the ground. Firing at what they thought was a colony of free Hork-Bajir.

A hologram.

Erek the Chee had created the illusion. And now, as the Yeerks fired, he created the illusion of Hork-Bajir burning, falling, dying.

But the laws of physics could not be denied.

The massive Dracon energies were not descending deep into a valley. They were hitting the mountain peak, only a hundred feet from us.

CRRRRRRR-ACK!

The ground shuddered.

And suddenly, the ground was falling away. A crack in the very rock itself.

A huge fissure opened up.

I staggered to my feet, crippled by the pain of my wound.

The fissure had separated us. Visser Three, and now an army of rushing, eager Hork-Bajir-Controllers on one side. Rachel and Tobias trapped there with them.

I was on the other side of the fissure. So was Visser One. My mother. We were alone.

She stood with her back to the cliff, raging.

"Too late, Visser Three! Too late to stop me!" Then, calling into her communicator, "Detach a fighter to get me off this rock!"

Rachel and Tobias were back against their own dead drop. Hork-Bajir hemmed them in, attacking relentlessly.

In seconds, it would be over.

All over. My plan. Done. Failed. Rachel and Tobias would die. Visser Three would live. And Visser One?

Out of the corner of my eye I saw a Bug fighter roaring out of the sky, rocketing down toward us.

I turned to face her. Visser One. The leader of the initial invasion of Earth.

She stared at me. She moved to aim the weapon at me.

I lowered my head and felt the power in my legs.

It would be a hundred-foot drop.

<I love you,> I whispered. And then, I lunged.

"The boy!" she whispered, amazed. "It's the boy!"

CHAPTER 29

I lunged.

The Dracon beam moved. Her finger tightened.

Too slow. She was too slow. I would hit her a split second before she could fire. I would hit her with all the power I possessed and she would fly backward into emptiness and —

RRRRROOOOOAAAARRR!

A flash of orange and black. It appeared over the lip of the cliff.

So fast!

The tiger hit me. Claws retracted, it hit me in my side and knocked me off my feet.

Spinning, I saw the Dracon weapon aimed right at me, following me, ready to fire.

And then, from the sky a bird dropped, wings folded back, talons out. It slashed at Visser One's face.

"Aaaarrggh!" she cried.

She clutched at bloody tracks on her cheeks.

She staggered back.

<Mom!> I cried.

For a horrible long moment she teetered on the edge, fighting gravity. I leaped up, racing to grab her, pull her back, somehow, save her.

But the tiger wrapped a massive arm around me and held me down.

She fell. Disappeared from sight.

<No! No! No!> I cried.

<Hang on, Marco,> Jake said. <Hang on, man. Hang on, man.>

He held me that way, pinned down. The strength of his tiger morph made my own strength insignificant.

<Hang on, Marco. Hang on, man.>

Dimly, as though I was watching it on an out-of-focus TV, I was aware that battle raged on the opposite peak.

I knew that more Hork-Bajir had joined the battle. I knew that an Andalite was leading them. That they were pushing back the tide of the Visser's troops.

The free Hork-Bajir. Ax had brought them from the real colony, miles away.

In the sky a battle raged between the Empire ship and the Blade ship with its fighters. Not my problem anymore.

Nothing was my problem. All I had to do was listen to the voice in my head saying, <Hold on, Marco. Hold on, man. Hold on.>

CHAPTER 30

I stayed in bed for most of the next week. Sick. At least that's what I told my dad.

I lay there staring at soap operas and Jerry Springer and old movies.

I didn't know how I'd gotten down off that mountain or made it home. I was gone during all that. Gone to a place in my head.

Jake came and saw me. He told me how Cassie had seen Visser Three's limo pulling in. They'd realized they were trapped. They'd gone at emergency speed back to roach morphs.

They figured nothing was going to kill a roach.

Cassie had been all the way into morph before Visser Three fried the car. Jake had only been halfway morphed. He'd been hurt, burned, unconscious.

Cassie had stayed to care for him, bringing him back to consciousness at the last minute. Just in time to demorph.

Jake had been seconds away from a lifetime trapped as something half roach, half human.

I listened to what he had to say. Listened to how Visser Three had escaped. How the free Hork-Bajir had lost five of their people in the battle.

I didn't care.

He went away and I flipped the channels with my remote control.

Two more days passed and Rachel came to see me. She sat in my chair and put her feet up on my desk.

"There's no body," she announced.

"What?" I asked distractedly. I flipped through a dozen more channels.

"Visser One. Your mother. I searched. In eagle morph. There's no body."

I felt my insides tighten.

"The Yeerks cleaned up their mess. Destroyed the evidence."

She shook her head. "No. The Yeerks Draconed the corpses. There are burn marks all over that hill. But nothing down where your mother fell."

The scene flashed back, another channel on the TV: the "my mother falling to her death" show. I saw her fall, slow-motion.

I saw the Bug fighter roaring past.

Could it have reached her?

No. Impossible.

"Nice try, Rachel," I said.

She shrugged. "I'm telling you what I saw. I wouldn't lie."

"Sure you would," I said. "Pity. Charity. Make Marco feel better."

"No. Because it won't make you feel better. It wouldn't be pity or charity. I wouldn't be doing you a favor. You've cried and yelled and hated yourself. It's bad, but if she's dead at least it would be over. If she's alive . . ."

I didn't say anything. She sighed and got up to leave. She touched the doorknob and I said, "Rachel? I was going to do it. Then I wasn't. I was trying to kill her. And save her. What do you do?"

"Do?"

"What do you do when you have to make a decision, and each choice is horrible? What would you do, Rachel? If it was your mom or dad or sisters. What would you do, Xena?"

"Me?" She sighed. "I guess I'd hope that someone would come along and take that decision away from me."

"Like Jake did to me."

"Yeah."

"What if she isn't dead? What if she really did survive? Oh, God, what if there's a next time?"

Rachel came back and sat beside me on the bed. She didn't hug me. Rachel's not a hugger. But she sat there with me.

"One battle at a time, Marco. One battle at a time."

Not much of an answer. But the only answer I had.

"Try the movie channel," Rachel said.

I aimed the remote control.

Don't miss

#31 The Conspiracy

I came around the corner after school and saw a taxi parked out in front of my house.

My mother shot across the porch, suitcase banging against her knees, and hurried down the sidewalk to the cab.

What the . . . ?

My mom didn't take cabs. Nobody around here did.

Everybody had cars.

"Mom!" I yelled, jogging over. "What happened?"

Because something had definitely happened.

I mean, I've seen my mom sniffle at Save the Children infomercials and Hallmark cards, but I can't remember the last time I ever saw her really cry.

But she was crying now.

Something must have happened to Tom.

Or to my dad.

My knees went weak and wobbly.

Funny, how even when your whole life has shifted into a daily *Twilight Zone* episode, there are still some things that can make you panic.

"I left you a note on the fridge, Jake," she said, hefting her suitcase into the trunk and slamming it shut. "My flight leaves in an hour and the traffic —"

"Mom, *what happened*?" I blurted.

My voice was high and shrill, not exactly the voice of a fearless leader, as Marco would have pointed out, had he been there.

"Oh." She blinked away fresh tears. "Grandpa G died. His housekeeper Mrs. Molloy found him this morning. I'm meeting your grandparents and we're driving out to Grandpa G's cabin to make the funeral arrangements."

"Grandpa G's dead?" I echoed, trying to wade through the emotions whirling around in my head.

Grandpa G. Not Tom. Not my father.

"Yes. His poor heart just gave out," she said.

"You're going to the cabin?" I said. "What about us?"

"You'll be coming out as soon as your father clears his work schedule," she said, touching my shoulder, forcing a brief smile, and sliding into the back seat. "He'll tell you about it. Everything will be fine. Make sure your suit is clean. I'll call when I get to Grandma's. I gotta go, honey."

She slammed the door and waved.

I watched as the cab disappeared around the corner.

Now what?

I headed into the house. Checked the scrawled note stuck under an apple magnet on the fridge.

Yeah. Grandpa G was dead.

According to Mrs. Molloy, who'd talked to the doctor, his heart had stopped while he was putting jelly on a slice of toast. He'd never even gotten a chance to eat it.

I shivered.

I'd cared about Grandpa G and now he was gone, and my family was smaller.

I didn't like that.

The kitchen door burst open. Tom stormed into the room.

"And I'm telling you, Dad, I can't go!" he snapped, tossing his books onto the table and scowling at me. "What're you looking at?"

"You're home early," I said, surprised.

My father plodded in, weary, harassed, and closed the door behind him.

"So are you," I said, glancing from him to Tom. "Did Mom tell you guys about Grandpa G?"

"Yes," my father said. "I was hoping to get here in time to take her to the airport but the traffic was terrible. I saw Tom walking home and picked him up."

"Did you know we're supposed to go out to the cabin?" Tom demanded, glaring at me like it was somehow my fault.

"Uh, yeah," I said cautiously, trying to figure out what his problem was. "So?"

"So, Tom's already informed me that he doesn't want to leave his friends to attend his great-grandfather's funeral," my father said, looking at Tom, not me. "However, he doesn't have a choice. We're going. All of us."

"When?" I said, feeling like I was missing something important. It was there but I just couldn't grab it.

"We're driving up Saturday morning," my father said.

"Dad, I can't," Tom insisted. "The Sharing's expecting me to help out this weekend. I gave them my word!"

"Well, you'll just have to explain that something more important came up," my father said. "I thought The Sharing was about promoting family values, right? Well, we're going to pay our respects to Grandpa G as a family."

"Dad, you don't understand!" Tom argued desperately.

Why was Tom so dead set against going out to the lake?

Okay, so it was boring. Grandpa G's cabin was the only house on the lake. His closest neighbor had been Mrs. Molloy and she lived seven miles away, halfway to town.

The only other house around was an old, abandoned hunting lodge across the lake.

No cable. No Taco Bell. No streetlights or crowds.

No movies. No malls . . .

No Sharing. No Yeerks . . .

"Uh, Dad?" I said. "How long are we staying?"

"It depends on the funeral. I'll write notes so you'll be excused from school through Tuesday of next week —"

"What?" Tom's eyes bulged in shock. "Tuesday? Dad, no way! Four days? I can't stay away for four days!"

"You can and you will," my father said, losing patience. "We're going as a family and that's final."

Tom's throat worked. His hands clenched into fists.

And for one, brief second I had the crazy thought that he was going to attack my father.

And oh man, even though I couldn't morph in front of them, I could feel the surge of adrenaline that came right before a fight.

Three, maybe four days. The maximum time a Yeerk can last without a trip to a Yeerk pool is three days. Four days without Kandrona rays and the Yeerk in Tom's head would starve.

Starve, Yeerk. Starve.

"It won't be that bad, Tom," I heard myself pipe up. "The lake's nice, remember?"

It broke the stalemate.

Tom looked at me. "You're an idiot, you know that?"

He was playing his role as condescending big brother. I was playing my role, too.

Starve, Yeerk. Die in agony, die screaming, Yeerk.

"Shut up," I said. "I'm not the one who's being a big baby about leaving."

I said it to annoy him and to bring us back to the rhythm we knew, the kind of normal sniping I could handle.

Because the hatred in Tom's eyes when he'd looked at my father had scared me.

And the hatred that had flared up in me, the hatred of the Yeerk, the sick thrill of anticipating its pain, had scared me, too.

"That's because you have no life," Tom sneered.

"Oh right, and you do?" I shot back.

"More than you'll ever know," he said darkly, distracted now.

"Enough," my father said. "I'm going to change. When I get back we'll order pizza. How does that sound?"

"I'm not hungry," Tom muttered, staring at the floor.

I wasn't either but my father was looking at me expectantly, so I said, "Pizza, I'm there."

My father nodded, satisfied, and left.

I gave my brother a look of sympathy, making peace. "Maybe you can get out of it, someway."

I had to fight to keep the sneer off my face. *Or maybe, Yeerk, your cover is falling apart, maybe you'll have to choose between keeping Tom and keeping your filthy life.*

"Shut up," Tom said absentmindedly. The Yeerk had no use for me, no interest in me. I was dismissed. Irrelevant.

I turned and blasted out into the backyard, my mind already buzzing with the possibilities.

Tom's Yeerk was trapped. Under pressure. Squeezed. It wasn't ready for this turn of events. Didn't know how to play it out. Didn't know what to do.

An opportunity? Maybe. Yeah, maybe.

Die, Yeerk.

Have you experienced the changes online?

TM

Up-to-the-minute info
on the Animorphs!

Sneak previews
of books and
TV episodes!

Contests!

Fun downloads
and games!

Messages from
K.A. Applegate

See what other fans
are saying on the Forum!

Check out the official Animorphs Web site at:
www.scholastic.com/animorphs

It'll change the way you see things.